THE W... PAPERS

Volume 3

OUTSMART

Daniel Parker

AVON BOOKS
An Imprint of HarperCollins*Publishers*

Outsmart

Printed in the United States of America.

For information address
HarperCollins Children's Books, a division of
HarperCollins Publishers, 1350 Avenue of the Americas, New York,
NY 10019.

 Produced by 17th Street Productions,
an Alloy, Inc. company
151 West 26th Street, New York, NY 10001

Library of Congress Catalog Card Number: 2001118925
ISBN 0-06-440794-2

First Avon edition, 2002

AVON TRADEMARK REG. U.S. PAT. OFF.
AND IN OTHER COUNTRIES,
MARCA REGISTRADA, HECHO EN U.S.A.

Visit us on the World Wide Web!
www.harperteen.com

OUTSMART

**Once Again, Some Important
Documents to Review . . .**

Hey Sunday,

I got your note. Don't worry about anything, okay? Burwell can't push us around. He's a burnt-out, bitter old freak. He actually thinks he can salvage his noncareer by recruiting rats to bust "troublemakers." YOU hold the aces. Not him.

By the way, Burwell never found the stationery. I still have it.

Don't you see? Olsen and Winnie don't know that we caught them. As soon as we figure out what they're doing, we'll go public. We'll change the school. Forever. Just like we promised in the Manifesto. On a massive scale. This is war! Today's swine is tomorrow's sausage!

Dear Phil,

I know you're at the game right now. I tried to e-mail you, but the school's server is down. I'll be brief. I can't go on with this. I can't live with the shame and guilt. Keep my share of the money, please. Just let me come clean with Noah. He deserves to know the truth. . . .

Dear Winnie,

How's it going, old buddy?

I know you're at the game right now (Go, Warriors!), but I thought I'd take this moment to give you an update on how our little pump-and-dump operation is going. . . .

Chet Thomas's Visi-Tech Returns
Initial investment: $4,000.00
Number of shares: 533
Initial stock value: $7.50 per share
Current value: $2.63 per share
Net profit: - $2,598.21

So as you can see, your projections were slightly optimistic. According to you, we should have made close to $177,000.00 by now. That means you were off by $179,598.21. Now, I'm not trying to assign any blame here. You know that I respect your talents enormously. I see you as a mentor in this field: a Socrates to my Plato, a Madonna to my Britney Spears.

. . . The PBs are a priority. Their behavior is growing increasingly erratic. Once they're out of the picture, the mess should be easier to clean up—although we still have to concern ourselves with all the alums who placed bets. I'm sure they're thinking I swindled them and threw the game on purpose, that I lied about betting for Wessex. The spread was too big in CM's favor. . . .

I'll handle the PBs. You handle Sal. And DON'T EVER WRITE TO ME AGAIN.

"O, from this time forth, my thoughts be bloody, or be nothing worth!" —*Hamlet*, Scene IV, Act IV

Dear Fred,

How are you? I am fine.

Let me qualify that. I _feel_ fine, even though I shouldn't. You see, by the time you get this, I will be on my way to a bright future of failure and misery. That's right.

I was kicked out, Fred. And it happened in no small part thanks to you. Much appreciated, buddy!

Phil,

Great game, huh, prick? You might want to think about giving up this hobby of yours. Because when you promise somebody you're going to deliver 200 pizzas and then you don't, you leave a lot of people hungry. I got a family to feed, Phil. You know my family. When they get hungry, they get grouchy. Remember that New York City councilman? The Greek guy? He sidelined in the pizza business, too. Then he screwed up a bunch of deliveries. Now nobody can find him. He must have moved away.

You got until Saturday. Unless you want to lose something valuable.

Part I
"The Beard" (Without the Beard)

1

Under normal circumstances, Sunday Winthrop supposed, there would be something comical about breaking into her own summer house.

Say, for instance, if it actually *was* summer, and she and her boyfriend (or whatever Fred Wright was—"boyfriend" was as close a label as any) had decided to sneak away from a party at Allison Scott's place for a little quality private time—now *that* would be comical. Or maybe it wouldn't be so much comical as weird. Well, actually, no, it wouldn't be either, because Fred would never be invited to a party at Allison Scott's place, no matter what the season. Not unless he was "the help."

Okay. Bad example.

Sunday watched Fred as he crouched in the darkness

7

by the back door, furiously jimmying the lock with a Swiss Army knife.

Were Swiss Army knives stronger than nail files? Yes. Of course they were. They had to be. Fred had learned his lesson when they'd broken the nail file in Olsen's rolltop desk. He wouldn't risk another fiasco like that. Not after all they'd been through tonight. He was a smart and sensible person. Wasn't he? Well, no. No, he wasn't. And neither was Sunday. Smart and sensible people would have stayed out of this . . . this . . . *nightmare.* Or morningmare. It was officially Sunday morning, after all. The sun would be coming up soon.

Sunday hovered over him, shivering. The wind coming off the ocean was ice cold. She was sweaty, though. Of course, that was probably due to the lingering horror of having witnessed a double murder. Not that she was an expert in psychology or anything.

"This place really doesn't have an alarm?" Fred whispered.

"My mom thinks an alarm system would make the house less quaint," Sunday said. Her voice was hoarse. She sounded more like a seventy-year-old man than a seventeen-year-old girl. But then, she'd slept maybe a total of five hours in two days. Better just to keep her mouth shut. She wasn't exactly in any condition to be making chitchat, anyway.

Fred pulled the knife from the keyhole and turned the knob. It fell off.

"Whoops. Sorry about that."

Sunday frowned. "Does that mean we can't get in?"

"No, I think I got the lock," he said.

Fred grabbed the broken stub and twisted it. The door creaked open.

The little entryway was still a mess from the summer, littered with old beach towels and badminton rackets and fly-fishing boots. The cleaning staff must have forgotten about this area. Or maybe they were just procrastinating until spring. They had until Memorial Day of next year to get the whole house back in shape. No member of the Winthrop family ever showed up during the off-season—which was precisely why Sunday had come here to hide. It was safe.

Well, maybe "safe" was pushing it. But it was out of the way. East Hampton was a good hundred and fifty miles from Wessex, at least.

Fred closed the door behind them. Sunday stood there for a moment, breathing in the salty odor that still clung to all the junk. Her heart stirred painfully. It *smelled* like summer in here . . . summer, when her biggest worry had been whether or not Allison was going to buy the same Prada beach bag that Sunday herself had ordered—

"Sunday? Aren't you going to turn on the lights?"

"Oh. Sorry." Sunday fumbled for the light switch. "Follow me," she said. She headed for the living room. The first sign of daybreak—a faint, luminous blue on the horizon—had already appeared in the huge bay windows that overlooked the ocean.

"Jeez," she muttered. "What time is it, anyway?"

"Five-fifteen," Fred said. He turned on the rest of the lights.

Sunday stopped short when she saw her reflection in the glass. *Yikes.* Things were worse than she'd thought. She'd never considered herself to be all that self-absorbed or shallow—at least, no more so than any other Wessex Academy Alumni Brat. But somehow, the bedraggled figure staring back at her from the windows, that haggard waif with the stringy black hair and the pea coat and the sweatpants . . . somehow, *that* frightened her even more than having watched a real-life Mafia hit.

"Sunday?" Fred rushed up beside her. "What is it? Do you see somebody out there?" He shoved his face against one of the panes of glass, cupping his hands around his eyes.

"No," she said. "Not out there."

Fred kept looking. Sunday found herself staring at his butt.

Good Lord. Things really *were* worse than she'd thought. She was losing it. Why did fear have such a freakish effect on her libido? True, Fred didn't look so bad. He'd borne the horrors of the night with a little more grace than she had. His brown hair was tousled; he was thin—actually, any thinner and he'd disappear—but his skin still had a healthy glow. He must have pulled a lot of all-nighters before. Or maybe he was just used to stress. He *was* a star basketball player, after all. Weren't athletes supposed to be impervious to pressure? Especially great ones? Yeah. And in a twisted way, *that*—Fred's talent, Fred's greatness, Fred's *fire*—was at the bottom of whatever miserable scam Headmaster Olsen and Winslow Ellis and Sal Viverito and whoever else were trying to pull. . . .

Ugh. Well, at least she didn't feel so amorous anymore. She felt sick.

"I don't think Sal could have followed us," Fred said. He sounded as if he were trying to convince himself more than her. He started pacing around the room. "I mean, he didn't see us at the quarry. At least, I don't think he did. He drove away pretty fast, you know? He was long gone by the time we split. I think he was just trying to get away from the scene of the crime."

Sunday shrugged. She didn't know what to say. Or maybe she was just done talking.

She slumped down into one of the wicker couches. She'd forgotten how comfortable this furniture was, especially the plaid pillows, sewn in the shape of sea bass. The whole design scheme was kind of ironic, too, because Mom had gone with a wicker living-room set—custom made by a local craftsman, no less—to give the house a rustic feel. She didn't want their house to be as "modern" as some of the others around here (read: "tacky"—although Mom would never insult her neighbors with such a pejorative term). In reality, though, the only quaint or rustic feature of the house was that it was still wired for regular cable. Everybody else on Lily Pond Lane had upgraded to DirecTV.

"I mean, I guess if he saw us, he could have waited for us out by the highway," Fred said, as if he and Sunday were having a conversation. "But there's no way he could have known we were coming *here*. I mean, worst case scenario: He somehow spotted us, then followed us to the New Farmington station and saw us get on a train to New York. But he wouldn't have seen us switch trains at Penn Station. Well, maybe. But he wouldn't have known that we were taking a train to East Hampton." He stopped and glanced at her. "Right? Right?"

"I-I don't . . ." Sunday had barely heard him. Her voice caught in her throat. She was still thinking about Mom. And that was stupid, because it only reminded her of the fact that Mom and Dad were sound asleep in Greenwich, without the slightest inkling that Sunday and Fred had run away from school. Or that Sunday was still even *seeing* Fred. Or that Headmaster Olsen was mixed up in gambling and pornography, or that these crimes had somehow gotten Noah Percy expelled and two teachers murdered by a hit man—yes, a *hit man*: a chubby, redheaded oaf who was not only a Wessex alum but, coincidentally, Fred's ex-girlfriend's boyfriend—

"Do you think the cops are looking for Burwell and Miss Burke yet?" Fred asked.

Sunday sighed. "Maybe," she said. "I don't know. I'm sure Olsen doesn't want it leaking out to the public that two teachers are missing. But Burwell is your dorm adviser. Don't you think some of the other kids in Ellis might have gotten worried when he didn't come home last night to check them in?"

"Maybe." Fred shrugged. "They were probably just psyched, though. It would give them all an excuse to sneak out or get wasted or whatever."

That was a good point. Ellis was a senior boys' dorm, and senior boys weren't exactly notorious worriers—especially when it came to somebody like Burwell (rest in peace), who had the unfortunate flaw of being both an absolute moron and a strict enforcer of the rules.

"Miss Burke is the dorm adviser in Meade Hall, though," Sunday said. "I mean, she *was.* I bet some of those sophomore girls freaked out when *she* didn't show. And maybe they called their parents. Maybe some of their parents called the cops. And if the cops know . . . then I bet other people know, too."

Fred sat down across from her. "And so they'll probably start looking for us. Once they realized that *we* aren't there, either. You know?"

"Yeah," Sunday said. She shivered again. She knew that by "they," Fred wasn't just talking about the cops, or even the school administration. He was also talking about Sal. And Sal's "family." The Mafia.

The Mafia.

She could hardly say the words to herself. They were too ridiculous. The Mafia wasn't even supposed to *exist* anymore. These days, organized crime was supposed to be controlled by the Colombians and the Russians and the Chinese. Or, at least, that was what she'd seen once on one of those special two-part episodes of "Law and Order."

"Maybe we should call the cops," Fred suggested. "Maybe we should just come clean and tell them what we saw. We'll just call them up and say, look, Paul Burwell and Patricia Burke are in the pond at the bottom of the quarry outside New Farmington, near Highway 91, and Salvatore Viverito put them there—" He stopped. He suddenly looked nause-ated. Sunday could guess why. He was probably thinking the same thing that *she* was: namely, that ratting Sal out to the cops was probably about the quickest way to ensure that the two of them would end up joining Burwell and Miss Burke—figura-tively, for sure, and maybe literally, as well. That pond was big enough for all of them. For all Sunday knew, the Viverito family disposed of *all* their vic-tims there.

"I think calling anybody would be a big mis-take," Sunday said. "At least for right now."

Fred nodded. "Yeah. Yeah, you're right."

Sunday blinked and rubbed her eyes. All at once, she was overcome with exhaustion. But hey, that was what running from the Mob could do to you, right? Ha, ha, ha. Too bad Noah wasn't here right now. He would appreciate her sense of humor. She stretched out on the couch. She had to sleep. Anything to escape. At this point, even one of Walker Crowe's carrot-sized joints might tempt her. So long as she didn't have to face reality.

"Hey, mind if I check the fridge?" Fred asked.

"Be my guest. The kitchen is through that big door. Help yourself to whatever. I doubt we have much, though. We always clean everything out at the end of the summer."

"That's okay," Fred said. "I'm good at scrounging."

How can you be hungry? Sunday wondered. No, the question was: How could she possibly fool herself into thinking that she could fall asleep? Closing her eyes didn't do a bit of good. It just made her very conscious of how fast her heart was pounding. Her mind spun with a rapid-fire barrage of hazy and unrelated images: Burwell's double-breasted suits, Allison's Sven Larsen potpourri, Winnie's plastic smile, Olsen's too-tight basketball uniform, Mackenzie's new TV-VCR . . . but again and again, she kept coming back to one little sequence: (1) Sal, hunching over Burwell's beat-up old Chevy; (2) the beat-up Chevy rolling down the embankment and plunging over the side of the quarry; (3) the look on Fred's face when the car hit the water—

"Hey, Sunday?" Fred called. "Are you sure that nobody comes here in the off-season?"

"Yeah. Why?"

"Have you ever had squatters?"

"Squatters?" Sunday sat up straight. "What do you mean?"

"You better come check this out."

She jumped off the couch and hurried to the kitchen.

Jesus. Somebody had definitely been here. Today,

by the looks of it. The table was set for one person, complete with a used napkin, a ketchup-smudged plate, and a crystal highball glass that looked as if it had been just recently filled with milk. It was disgusting. Who knew that the cleaning staff took such advantage of the place? The counter was a disaster area, as well, strewn with dirty bowls and open cereal boxes and about a dozen packets of those 33-cent ramen noodles. She couldn't help but laugh. For some reason, she'd always assumed that the only people who ate those noodles were boarding-school kids—because you had to be either incredibly cheap, lazy, or stoned to do it. They had the nutritional value of cardboard.

"What's so funny?" Fred asked.

"Nothing," Sunday said. She shook her head. "It's just . . . well, judging from their taste in food, I wouldn't be surprised if the cleaning people graduated from Wessex."

Fred stepped forward and peered at the highball glass. His nose wrinkled. "Man," he said. "You guys might want to think about hiring somebody else."

"That's exactly what Allison said this past summer," Sunday said. "Well, not exactly. She said it in harsher terms." Her smile faded. Actually, the conversation was still fresh in her memory. Very fresh.

It had taken place on the beach. Allison had gotten

upset over the fact that the Winthrops used a no-
name valet service, as opposed to Hampton Valets,
"the only competent service in the area." (Allison's
words, not Sunday's.) Sunday had made the mistake
of asking "Who cares?"—and after several minutes of
stupid and pointless arguing, Allison had stormed
off in a huff. To reject Hampton Valets was to reject
everything that she stood for: tradition, quality, and
the Establishment. To embrace No-Name was to
embrace degeneracy. She hadn't said it quite like
that, of course, but she was *thinking* it. And it was just
about this time that Sunday had begun to dread (yes,
really, truly *dread*) the idea of being Allison's room-
mate, of spending another year at Wessex, of being
trapped in this absurd existence where people genuinely believed that your housecleaning service said
something about you as a person. . . .

"Sunday?" Fred asked.

"Yeah?"

"Why are you crying?"

Sunday sniffed. Tears were streaming down her
cheeks. She hadn't even noticed. "I guess . . . I just . . .
I don't know."

Fred took her hand and gave it a gentle squeeze.
"We'll be all right. We'll get through this," he said.
"Okay?"

"Yeah. I know." She wiped her eyes. She was

lying, though. She knew exactly why she was crying, and it wasn't because she was worried that they weren't going to get through this—whatever "this" was. (And she *was* worried. In fact, "worried" was pretty much the understatement of the decade.) No, she was crying because she'd never known until this very moment how wonderful it was to be trapped in that absurd existence—the very thing she'd railed so vehemently against in the Manifesto of SAFU—where her biggest goal of the day was to get Allison to shut up so she could just enjoy the sun and the ocean and the beautiful, crazy, boring, ridiculous life she led.

Because now that life was over.

At around eight o'clock in the morning, Sunday decided to trek into town for food—*real* food, as opposed to sugar-coated cereal and ramen noodles. Anything was better than sitting around that big, creepy, empty beach house. It was clear that neither she nor Fred would be getting any sleep. So once again, she slithered into her pea coat and headed out into the cold. Fred decided to tag along. He wasn't in any shape to be by himself.

East Hampton was really pretty pleasant in the off-season, Sunday realized. No tourists, no traffic, none of those overpriced antique stands—nothing. The flat, sandy roads were deserted. And aside from the wind and the lonely cry of an occasional seagull, the whole town was perfectly silent. It was a good thing, too. Sunday needed silence. She needed to think. She shivered, wrapping her arms around her sides. Fred stared at the pavement as he walked.

"I gotta talk to Noah," he mumbled.

"What do you mean?"

"He still thinks *I'm* the one who got him kicked out," Fred said. "And no matter what happens, I have to let him know what really went down. Even if it . . . you know, even if it's risky."

Uh-oh. Sunday could sense a bad idea percolating in Fred's brain. Definitely. Fred was nodding to himself—that same way he'd nodded to himself the night he'd suggested breaking into Olsen's house in the middle of a nor'easter.

"I thought we weren't going to call anybody," she said.

Fred shook his head. "I'll call him from a pay phone in town. That way, you know, if anybody is tapping your phone or anything . . ."

Sunday swallowed. "Why would anybody tap my phone?"

"They wouldn't," Fred said quickly. "I'm just saying if they *did*. But, you know, also . . . in case Noah asks where we're calling from, and we don't

want to tell him, he can't star-sixty-nine us to figure out where we are."

Suddenly Sunday was very nervous. *Star-sixty-
nine? Figure out where we are?* Were people looking for
them already? Actually . . . of course they were.
People must have started looking for them last
night, when she and Fred hadn't been in their
dorms for check-in . . . *oh, man.* This was bad.
Olsen would have definitely been notified about an
absent AB. Which meant he would have called
Sunday's parents. Which meant that Mom and Dad
weren't sleeping comfortably in Greenwich; they were
frantic with worry. And who knew what they would
do to find her? Maybe making a phone call wasn't
such a bad idea. At the very least, Sunday could just
let her parents know that she was *alive.* For now,
anyway.

"You know, there's something we haven't talked
about," Fred said.

"What's that?"

Fred paused at the intersection of Lily Pond
Lane and Ocean Avenue. "We haven't talked about
why Sal killed Burwell and Miss Burke," he whispered.

Sunday nodded. She looked out at the rolling
waves. "I think he did it as a warning."

"A warning? To who?"

"To Olsen," she said, turning back to Fred. "I mean, you read the note Sal left him. 'You got until Saturday. Unless you want to lose something valuable.' Olsen must have screwed him in some way. The 'valuables' he lost were Burke and Burwell."

Fred's face went pale.

"What is it?" Sunday asked.

"I think I know exactly how Olsen screwed him. Remember that letter Hobson's dad wrote? The one where he compared me to a chimp? He said that he wanted to bet twenty grand on Wessex in the game against Carnegie Mansion. He was betting on *me*, Sunday. And so was Olsen, and who knows how many others. That's why everybody made such a big deal about the game. When I screwed up, it cost them . . ." Fred squeezed his eyes shut. "Jesus. It's my fault. This whole thing is my fault. Burwell and Miss Burke would still be alive if it weren't for me."

Sunday took his arm. "Fred, don't say that. This has nothing to *do* with you. I mean, it has as much to do with you as Olsen's Bill Wilson fetish has to do with you."

"Bill Walton," Fred said.

"Whatever. The point is, the connection is there, but it's kind of like the connection between award shows and really ugly ten-thousand-dollar dresses. Sure, they're related, but one isn't to blame for the other. You know what I mean?"

Fred didn't answer.

"Okay, bad example. Forget it. What *I* want to know is about Operation Time Capsule. See, the way I figure it, Olsen was planning to cover his bets with the money he wants to get from Noah—"

Sunday's stomach plummeted. In that instant, she completely forgot what she'd just been talking about. Out of the corner of her eye, she spotted a bright red Camaro. It was coming from the town center, driving slowly toward them down Ocean Avenue.

"What?" Fred asked. He turned, following her gaze.

"Come on!" Sunday hissed. She tugged on his arm and started sprinting back down Lily Pond Lane. In less than four seconds, Fred was already a good twenty feet in front of her. She'd never seen anyone run so fast. (Why couldn't *she* be a star athlete?) She refused to look over her shoulder. She figured the less she saw, the better. The old, ostrich's head-in-the-sand strategy. She kept her eyes glued on her house.

Halfway down the block, Fred slowed and turned around. "Hey," he panted. "Wait a sec. The car isn't following us. It turned around. It might not be Sal."

Sunday sped right past him. "Come on!" she barked.

"Maybe it's just a coincidence. Maybe that car—"

"Shut up and move!" Sunday commanded.

Without breaking stride, she hurtled over the fence on the edge of her property and dashed across the lawn to the back door. Fred was right on her heels. Her lungs burned. Her heart was firing like a machine gun. Thank God they'd left the door open. They rushed inside and locked it behind them.

The inside knob fell off, too. It bounced on the concrete floor: *ping!*

"Dammit," Sunday hissed. Her voice quavered. She ran to the living room. "What should we do?"

"I don't know," Fred said. "The car took off, though. . . ."

Sunday froze. If her heart had been beating fast before, it was now ready to explode right out of her rib cage.

She and Fred weren't alone. Somebody was standing by the bay windows.

Fred stopped beside her. "Holy—"

It was Noah. *Noah Percy.*

He was . . . here.

But he seemed just as shocked as they did. His blue eyes were wide. He didn't look so great, actually. His normally fluffy curls were matted and greasy. He was also pretty much undressed—except for a pair of boxer shorts, an undershirt, and his tweed jacket. In one hand, he held a bowl of cereal. In the other, he held a spoon. A little drop of milk trickled down his chin.

Fred and Sunday looked at each other. Then they looked back at Noah.

"Howdy," he said.

Note left under
Headmaster Olsen's front door

Phil,

I guess you didn't believe what I said in my last letter. Too bad. I take that as an insult. That makes two insults in less than a month. Our biggest competitors insult us less than that.

First you expel my brother, which, I got to hand it to you, took real balls. I don't know what kind of message you were trying to send us, but we weren't too happy about it. Speaking of which, we'd like to have Tony readmitted. But that's a conversation for another time, and one you'll be having with my father, the don. That's a personal matter. Business comes first with our family. You know that.

I hate getting angry. Really. Anger makes it hard for a guy to think straight. I mean, you remember what I was like at school, don't you? I never so much as gave anybody a dirty look. Never raised my voice. Never called anyone a prick. I pretty much kept to myself. I didn't even want to make pizzas. School was school. That was the way my family wanted it. No business. In our family, we got a rule: Don't piss where you eat. In other words, don't mix business with personal stuff. (Believe me, it sounds a lot better in Italian.)

See, in case you forgot, <u>you</u> came to <u>me</u> about making pizzas. Remember that, Phil? Because if you don't, that's fine. I got the whole conversation on tape.

But that's another subject. You came to me because you thought the pizza business could make you a little extra cash. I can understand that. Who couldn't use some pocket change? The problem is, you got greedy. And now you got more problems. You got teachers who suddenly disappear for no reason. And when those teachers don't even bother to leave forwarding addresses or to make arrangements for substitutes to pick up their course loads or tend to their dorms . . . well, gee, Phil. People start to wonder. That's no way to run a school.

You got until noon Wednesday. Then things start getting <u>really</u> ugly.

Ciao.

2

For the first time in her life, Allison Scott was about to do the unthinkable.

She was about to *break the rules*.

Sadly, however, she didn't have a choice. Her former friends had driven her to it—one through the most heinous form of betrayal imaginable, and the other through . . . what? Through lunacy? Yes, that was as good a word as any. Only a lunatic would run away from school, leaving her roommates to fret all night long about her safety and possible whereabouts. Only a lunatic would compromise everything she was supposed to value—her education, her social standing, her entire *world*—for a sleazy fling with some thug from the streets of Washington, D.C.

In fact, *lunatic* was too kind a word for Sunday. It implied that she wasn't to be held responsible for her actions. And that wasn't the case. No. *Somebody* had to take *some* responsibility for *something* around here. The madness had gone on long enough. And Allison was going to put an end to it. Members of the Scott family didn't sit back and allow events to control them. Members of the Scott family *took* control—even if it meant committing an offense punishable by five days' suspension (as cited on page 18 of the Orientation Handbook, in the section regarding unsanctioned travel to and from campus).

"Hey, are you serious about this, Al? You're really just gonna take off and look for Sunday? Are you sure that's such a good idea?"

Allison ignored the questions. She simply continued folding her Chanel blouse and packing it into her Louis Vuitton bag. She ignored the questions because the person posing them was not worthy of a reply. That person—that *witch*, that *backstabber*—who was standing in the doorway like an idiot and staring at Allison with those annoying brown bug-eyes and chomping on bubble gum . . . *yuck*. That person was not worthy of any acknowledgment whatsoever. *None at all.* Because as of last night, Mackenzie Wilde had ceased to exist for Allison Scott. And

Allison Scott would never stoop to answer any of Mackenzie Wilde's stupid questions ever again. In fact, she could barely stand another second of being stuck in the triple with her. Which was one more excellent reason to leave and search for Sunday.

"Al, come on," Mackenzie pleaded. "You can't just go on giving me the silent treatment, okay? This is important. I mean, this is, like, life or death, you know? And I know you're still pissed about Hobson, and you have every right to be, but this is—"

"I wonder if I should bring my raincoat," Allison asked herself in a very loud voice. She marched to her closet and tore the coat off the hanger. *Life or death?* If she hadn't been grinding her teeth so hard, she might have laughed. Of all the ridiculous, overblown . . . well, Mackenzie had always had a flair for the dramatic. Allison had to give her that.

"I'm serious, Al," Mackenzie said. "A lot of bad stuff is going on. Stuff that you don't even know about. I swore I wouldn't tell, but, the thing is—"

There was a knock on the door.

Allison sighed crossly. "Who is it?" she called.

"Headmaster Olsen. May I come in?"

Mackenzie's face went white. Her gum fell out of her mouth. She started shaking her head. "No, no, no," she mouthed silently. "Don't do it!"

"Of course you can come in," Allison replied. What the hell was Mackenzie's problem, anyway? Allison brushed past her without a glance, carefully sidestepping the fallen Bubblicious as she strode into the triple's little common area. This could be good news. Maybe Olsen was bringing word that they'd found Sunday. Maybe breaking the rules wouldn't be necessary after all. She unlocked the door.

"Has Sunday shown up yet?" Olsen asked breathlessly.

"No," Allison muttered. She stepped aside and allowed him to come in. "I guess you haven't heard from her, either."

He shook his head and shambled inside. He looked terrible. And *smelled* terrible. He was so sweaty. The front of his button-down shirt was soaked. His comb-over had flopped to the wrong side, and the ratty hair dangled limply by his right ear, revealing a glistening red bald spot on top of his scalp. Clearly, he hadn't slept. (Then again, neither had she or Mackenzie—but at least they'd showered.) He was still wearing the same brown slacks and paisley bow tie he'd been wearing the night before.

"Listen, girls," he said. He paced the room, wringing his hands. "It's very important that we find Sunday as soon as possible. Her parents are very concerned."

Allison glanced at Mackenzie.

Mackenzie took a step back and slammed Allison's door: *smack!*

Headmaster Olsen jerked. He turned to Allison.

"Good heavens. Is Mackenzie all right?"

"Fine," Allison grumbled. "So, you talked to the Winthrops?"

"Yes, I did." He paused, studying the Sven Larsen black coffee table and black living-room bench. They were the only furnishings in the room, aside from Mackenzie's TV-VCR. To the undiscerning eye, they were very similar. Olsen opted to sit on the table.

"They have no idea where she could have gone," he continued. "They tried calling friends, relatives . . . even the Percys. They thought that she might have gone to see Noah. But apparently Noah is missing as well."

Allison's eyes narrowed. "Are you serious?"

"He disappeared after his dismissal."

"Really?" she gasped. She couldn't believe it. Sunday, Fred Wrong, Miss Burke, Mr. Burwell . . . and now Noah. All gone. Gone! Just like that. It was so bizarre, so *scandalous*. Of course, Noah's disappearance wasn't such a big surprise. Maybe he'd become a drifter, a hobo who slept under bridges. Why not? He'd lost his marbles a long time ago. Rumor even had it that he'd been kicked out for sleeping with Miss Burke and videotaping it. Not that Allison believed such tripe for a second . . . but still. Anything was possible where Noah Percy was concerned. Anything. But were his disappearance and Sunday's somehow connected? It couldn't be a coincidence. Not when *five* people were involved. Or could it?

Olsen stood up, apparently too distracted to keep still. He left a damp little spot in the shape of his behind on the table.

Eww. Allison would definitely have to disinfect that.

"Well, I'm going to go home and try to get some rest," Olsen said. He coughed and glanced at his watch. His wrist was trembling. "It's already almost nine in the morning."

"Headmaster Olsen? Are you sure you're all right? I mean, is there anything I can do?"

"No. Just . . . if you hear anything, please let me know. Immediately."

"I will," she said.

He paused at the door. "One more thing. Have you talked to Winslow Ellis lately?"

Blood rushed to Allison's face. Was that a not-so-veiled hint that Olsen had seen her and Winnie traipsing off to the Waldorf last night? Not that there was anything wrong with making out with somebody in the woods—not according to the Orientation Handbook, anyway. The faculty frowned upon such behavior, of course, but it wasn't specifically *forbidden*. It wasn't like smoking pot or having sex in a dorm room. Besides, as Olsen had said himself on a few occasions, everybody was entitled to a few minor rebellions every now and then. It was natural.

"I hung out with him last night for a little while," Allison admitted. "Why?"

"How did he seem to you?"

"How did he . . . *seem*?"

"Yes. Nervous, in any way? Anxious?"

She frowned. Come to think of it, Winnie *had* been acting a little funny. In fact, *he'd* asked Allison about *Olsen*. He'd asked her if Olsen ever pissed her off, or worried too much, or tried to come off as sounding "holier-than-thou." Then, just as mysteriously, he'd dropped it.

"Why?" she asked.

Olsen shook his head. "No reason," he muttered. "But if you see him, tell him that I'd like to talk to him as soon as possible."

"Okay. I will."

"Thank you, Allison." He flashed a brief, uncomfortable smile. "I know I can count on you." He opened his mouth as if to say something else, then hurried out the door.

Well. That visit had been unsettling, to say the least. Allison had never seen Olsen in such bad shape. He hadn't even quoted Shakespeare. Not once. In her whole entire life, she'd never had a single conversation with Olsen where he didn't slip in at least one pithy little phrase from *The Tempest* or *Othello* or whatever else.

Mackenzie poked her head out of Allison's room. "Is he gone yet?" she whispered.

Allison's face soured. She wasn't going to dignify that question with so much as a snort. She marched past Mackenzie and zipped up her luggage. It was time to find Sunday and figure out what the hell was going on, once and for all.

"Al, don't go, okay?" Mackenzie said. "Please. We have to talk. You can't trust Olsen. He's a Capricorn with Capricorn rising. I'm serious—"

"Will you *please* get out of my way?" Allison demanded, slinging the bag over her shoulder. Standing in Mackenzie's presence was one thing. But if she had to listen to one more second of astrological *crap* . . .

Mackenzie stepped aside, accidentally squashing the piece of bubble gum. "Whoops. Look, just be careful, okay? Please promise me that you'll be careful—"

Allison slammed the triple's door and hurried downstairs.

Outside, it was a beautiful, crisp autumn morning. The air felt clean. *Sharp.* Just like her resolve. She was going to be careful, all right—careful as in "meticulous." She would devote herself to finding Sunday Winthrop, whatever it took. Sunday couldn't hide forever. Allison knew the girl too well. There was only a certain number of places where she might go.

Sunday Winthrop just wasn't all that creative, original, or impulsive.

And if Allison *did* succeed in finding Sunday and returning her safely to campus (which she would), there was no doubt that she would receive some attention. Maybe even some notoriety off campus. And *that* fulfilled Golden Rule Addendum No. 2 of her Seven-Part Life Plan: Something is only worth doing if you can become famous for it.

Yes. Today was going to be a good day.

Before she headed off to the New Farmington train station, however, there was one last item of business to take care of. She had to find Winnie. She had to let him know that Olsen wanted to talk to him as soon as possible. Because that was part of her new resolve, as well: to do whatever Olsen asked of her, no matter how trivial or weird. After all, doing Olsen's bidding was the only way to ensure that she, too, like Winnie, would be put on that special committee that allowed students to use cell phones.

Then *she* would be in control. The way she ought to be.

"So Olsen seemed scared about something, huh?" Winnie asked.

Allison didn't trust herself to speak. Her mood had soured considerably since she'd left Reed Hall. *Considerably.* It had taken nearly an hour to track down Winnie (who on earth went to the Waldorf at nine o'clock on a Sunday morning?), and her back was killing her from having dragged her luggage all over campus. Add that to the fact that her jaw was aching . . .

"What did he say?" Winnie said.

"I *told* you," Allison snapped. "Nothing. Just that he wants to know where Sunday is, and that he wants to talk to you. As soon as possible."

"As soon as possible," he echoed. "Right, right."

Strange. If she hadn't known any better, she would have said that Winnie seemed scared about something, too. He kept pacing around the little clearing and wringing his hands—just like Olsen had. He was also extremely unkempt. His luxurious blond hair was a mess, and he was wearing a Wessex sweatsuit. Winnie *never* wore sweatsuits—with good reason. They weren't very flattering. He looked like an overweight stockbroker, like those fat Class of '88 guys who showed up at every alumni weekend and insisted on jogging around campus in groups—as if that would somehow erase the fact that they drank their weight in beer each night.

Something rustled in the dead leaves by the dry creek bed. Winnie jumped.

"It's a *squirrel*, Winnie," Allison muttered. "What's wrong with you, anyway?"

He shook his head. His typically rosy round cheeks were void of color. "Nothing. It's just . . . ah, well, I got some problems to take care of." He stopped pacing for a moment and smiled at her. "You know, I had fun last night, by the way."

Allison lowered her eyes. "Me, too," she murmured. *Oh, Winnie.* Now she felt bad. From a certain perspective, a sweatsuit might even be cute—in a teddy-bearish sort of way.

"So what's with the bag?" he asked. "Going somewhere?"

"I . . ." Allison thought for a moment. She should have considered the possibility that he might ask her that. She supposed she could just tell him the truth. He'd understand. On the other hand, he might want to come with her. No, it was best just to keep this little Sunday-finding operation to herself. Besides, he'd find out what she was up to sooner or later—either when she returned to campus with Sunday, or when Mackenzie blabbed to everyone that she had gone *looking* for Sunday, which was bound to happen some time very soon. The girl was incapable of keeping a secret. Although she *had* managed to hide her affair with Hobson for God knew how long . . .

"I can't say, Winnie," she said. "I'm sorry."

He frowned. "What do you mean, you can't *say*?"

"Winnie, please. Don't press me on this. If you want, I can make something up, but I don't like to lie." She gritted her teeth. Yes, she was through with lying. To lie was to be like Mackenzie. To lie was to be a devious, duplicitous *fraud*.

Winnie's eyes narrowed. "Wait a second. Does this have anything to do with Sunday?"

Allison blinked. "Of course not."

Winnie just kept staring at her.

"What?" said Allison.

"Nothing," he mumbled. He leaned against a tree and gazed off into the woods. "I'm sorry, Allison. I'm just a little edgy, that's all. I mean, people seem to be disappearing for no reason. You know? It's kind of scary. It's *really* scary. It's like some bad teen horror movie come to life. But we're actually living it."

"I know. I know." Allison sighed. She'd never realized it until recently, but he could get so philosophical when he was depressed. It was very sweet. And it was definitely a side of him that he tried too hard to conceal. "Look, I better go. Remember: don't forget to talk to Olsen. I'll call you as soon as I get back, okay?"

He turned and gave her a faint smile. "That's it?"

"What do you mean?"

"No good-bye kiss?" He arched one of his newly improved eyebrows.

She blushed. "Well, maybe just one." She stepped across the clearing and planted a quick peck on the side of his cheek.

"How about another?" he asked in a husky voice. Before she could answer, he wrapped his arms around her and started passionately kissing her neck, groping at her Louis Vuitton bag with his fleshy hands.

"Winnie!" she barked. "Stop it!" She wriggled free and shoved him against the tree.

He grinned at her, breathing heavily. "What?"

"What? *What?* For God's sake, it—it's . . . I haven't

even had brunch yet!" she stammered. "Anyway, I told you last night that second base was my limit. And I meant it."

"I know. But that was last night. I figured our relationship had progressed since then."

Allison glared at him. "That's not funny," she said.

Winnie opened his mouth again, but he was interrupted by a piercing *bee-bee-beep* from his crotch. His cell phone. Perfect. Just perfect! Allison shook her head and marched toward the path that led back to campus.

"Al, wait," he called. "Please." He yanked the phone out of his pocket and clicked it open. "Hello? Sal? Yeah, shut up for a second. . . . Al! Wait! I'm sorry!"

Sure, you're sorry, Allison thought miserably. *You're so sorry that you're laughing and taking calls.* She could hear him quite clearly back there over the *crunch-crunch-crunch* of her feet in the leaves, chatting away on the phone to this "Sal" person. What *was* it with teenage boys? Were they really that out-of-control? Totally helpless in the face of their own raging hormones? Winnie was an *Ellis*. His name carried weight. His name inherently implied honor and decency. He was supposed to respect women. He was supposed to be a gentleman. Did

41

anyone even care what the word *gentleman* meant anymore?

"Al, you don't understand!" Winnie shouted. "Stress makes me horny! I can't help it!"

So. There was her answer: Evidently not.

From: Undisclosed Sender
To: Undisclosed Recipient
Subject: SW, FW, and the PBs

I hear you're looking for me. What's going
on? Where is everyone?

From: Undisclosed Sender
To: Undisclosed Recipient
Subject: re: SW, FW, and the PBs

The PBs are gone. Our friend took care of
them for us. I saw the whole thing. I was
at the quarry, waiting for them to show up.
I was going to take care of them myself. It
was dark, but I saw PB1's Chevy go over the
side of cliff. Both PB1 and PB2 were inside.
It was awful, to say the least. When I got
back to campus, there was a note waiting for
me. Our friend wants his money. I suggest
that you get it to him ASAP. And FYI: NP is
missing as well.

From: Undisclosed Sender
To: Undisclosed Recipient
Subject: re: re: SW, FW, and the PBs

NP is missing? I don't understand.

From: Undisclosed Sender
To: Undisclosed Recipient
Subject: re: re: re: SW, FW, and the PBs

Yes, you do, you imbecile. He's GONE. Just
like the others. It's crucial that you get
our friend the money. I can't stress that
enough. And in the meantime, I think it
would behoove us both to find SW, FW, and
NP. You're friends with them, so I assume
you know where they might have gone. None of
their families seem to have any idea. I'm
concerned that they might report their
suspicions (whatever those suspicions may
be) to the authorities. I also suggest that
you delete these messages immediately, and
don't contact me again until you have
something of value to report. "The moment is
thy death. Away!"

Good God. Noah Percy hates my guts.

Fred swallowed. There was no denying it. *Look at him!* The guy was just sitting there across from Fred and Sunday, nestled in those ridiculous fish-shaped plaid pillows—stone rigid, poker-faced, silent. He hadn't even acknowledged Fred's existence. Not in over an hour. He would only look at Sunday—well, either Sunday or his bare feet. His undershirt might as well be printed with the words FRED WRIGHT MUST DIE.

The thing was, Fred had known that Noah would be pissed. But this was hard-core, especially for Noah. It didn't *fit.* Which said a lot, because in the six weeks that Fred had been a student at Wessex, he'd pretty much witnessed the full gamut of extreme human behavior—from the rotten and terrifying, to the criminal and ludicrous, to the downright baffling—but this . . . this *venom* that was etched into the lines around Noah's mouth and smoldering blue eyes . . . this was by far the most disturbing. In some ways, it was even more disturbing than Sal's murderous rampage. At least Sal was in the Mob. At least he had an excuse to be hateful and violent. But Noah didn't have a hateful or violent bone in his body. Not until now, anyway.

"So let me get this straight," Fred said. "You've been hiding out here at Sunday's summer house since you got expelled? For five whole days?"

Once again, Noah didn't respond. He just grabbed his half-eaten bowl of soggy cereal off the coffee table and stormed into the kitchen. "Hey, I'm sorry about the mess, Sunday," he called. "If I'd been expecting company, I would have cleaned up. Which reminds me: I know this may sound like a funny question, but what are *you* doing here?"

Sunday exchanged a quick glance with Fred. "It's . . . um, well, it's sort of a long story, Noah. Maybe you should just tell us why you didn't go home. Not that it's a big deal that you're here," she added quickly. "I'm just a little surprised. You know. That's all."

"Of course." Noah poked his head out the kitchen door. "I came here because, like I told you, I panicked.

I couldn't think of anywhere else to go. I also assumed that nobody would show up here in the off-season, which gave me a good seven months to max out all my credit cards and figure out what the hell I'm gonna do with my life, because I can't go home."

"Why not, exactly?" Fred asked.

The question seemed to break the spell. Noah finally turned his attention to Fred. The downside was that Noah's expression was very similar to the expression Coach Watts had worn at the end of the Carnegie Mansion game—one which stated in pretty unambiguous terms that Fred was a cockroach, fit only for extermination.

"I'll tell you," Noah spat. "I can't go home, *exactly*, because my parents disowned me, *exactly*, which means I don't even *have* a home, *exactly*." His face brightened. "And why is that? *You*." He thrust a finger at Fred. "Exactly!"

"Your parents disowned you?" Sunday cried.

Noah's arm dropped to his side. "Well, no," he muttered. "Not exactly. But they will."

"Have you talked to them?" Fred asked.

"What's the point? You don't know my dad, Fred. Actually, neither do I, really. But I *do* know that he's not the kind of guy who would accept a son in the home porn industry. He calls himself 'Big Bucks' Chuck. Everything has to be 'big bucks' with him—when he walks to the store, it's a 'big bucks' walk. So he'd probably only be psyched if my movie roles were 'big bucks' roles. Speaking of which, do you think you can get me any more porn gigs? You know, paying gigs this time? I'll start working out, I promise. I've actually got a pretty nice set of abs. Buns of steel, too. I really need the money, and if you set up the camera to get better shots—"

"Noah, Fred had nothing to do with that," Sunday interrupted. "He's been trying to *help* you. I swear to God."

Fred was very relieved that Sunday had decided to take charge of the conversation. Not so much because she was sticking up for him—though that was, of course, undeniably cool. No, he was just grateful that she'd managed to put an end to Noah's rant. Any more of it and Fred would have bolted from the house.

"Help me?" Noah laughed. "That's funny, Sunday. I never knew you were such a joker. But then, I never knew you had a secret infatuation with criminals—"

"I can prove it," Sunday insisted. "Look what we found in Olsen's office." She hopped off the couch and ran over to her pea coat, which was lying in the middle of the living-room rug. After a quick search of her pockets, she dug out a crumpled piece of notebook paper.

"Here." She handed it to Noah. "Read this."

OPERATION TIME CAPSULE

1998, GT, $75,000

Breakdown
PO: $25,000
WE: $25,000
PβB: $10,000
TR: $15,000

1999, WC, $100,000

Breakdown
PO: $35,000
WE: $35,000
PβB: $10,000
JL: $20,000

2000, MR, $125,000

Breakdown
PO: $50,000
WE: $50,000
PβB: $10,000
JH: $15,000

2001, NP, $200,000

<u>Breakdown</u>
PO: $100,000
WE: $100,000
Pβ1: N/A
Pβ2: N/A

NP – Noah
PO – Olsen
WE – Winnie
Pβ1 – Burke or Burwell
Pβ2 – Burke or Burwell

Noah frowned. Then he started laughing.

"What's so funny?" Sunday asked.

"You wrote this," he said. "This is your handwriting."

"So?"

He shoved the piece of paper back in Sunday's hands. "So it doesn't prove a thing, other than that you're very creative. *Very* creative. You should be proud. This is some piece of work: the initials, the money, the whole layout. And, I mean, 'Operation Time Capsule'? Come on. That's brilliant. You should be writing spy novels. Throwing Olsen into the mix was a nice touch, too. Mackenzie would be honored. Or . . . wait a sec. Was this Mackenzie's idea? She's always talking about evil plots and conspiracies."

Fred jumped to his feet. He couldn't stand it anymore. "Noah, this is *real*! Sunday found a typed version of that paper in Olsen's desk when we were looking for evidence that he set you up and blackmailed you. She just copied it so she could put the original back."

Noah nodded seriously. "Yeah, Olsen's desk can be pretty crazy. The last time I went through it, I found a bunch of home enemas. And the CliffsNotes to the complete works of Shakespeare. And an Afro wig with a chin strap. That thing is a treasure chest—"

"Why don't you believe us?" Sunday shouted. "Why don't you believe *me*? Come on. How long have we known each other, Noah? Since we were babies, right? And when have I ever lied to you? Huh? Name *one* time that I lied to you."

"One time. One time. Let me see. . . ." Noah scratched his chin.

"Noah," she groaned.

"I'm sorry." He looked down at his feet again. His tone softened a little. "Okay. You're right. I don't think you're a liar. It's just funny, though. You just said exactly what *I* said to Olsen the day he

51

kicked me out. He didn't believe me when I told him that *I* wasn't the one who, you know . . . made the tape. I asked him if he could think of one time I'd ever lied to him."

"What did he say?" Sunday asked.

"He told me that he wanted me out of his school, his office, and his life."

Sunday sighed.

"Okay," Noah said. "Say that I believe that Olsen is in on blackmailing me. Which, you have to admit, is kind of hard to believe." He glanced at Fred. "That doesn't mean that *he* isn't in on it."

Fred looked him in the eye. "Look, man. Even if you don't trust me, I know you trust Sunday. And she would never choose to screw over one of her best friends for a guy like me. If she thought I was involved, she'd have nothing to do with me. Not in a million years."

Noah just stared at him.

Fred's heart pounded. It was kind of funny. That was probably the closest he'd ever come to confessing his true feelings for Sunday. Not that he was even sure what those feelings were—other than that he thought she was hot (who didn't?), and that the uncanny way she kept topping herself in terms of brilliance and just plain *sexiness* never failed to set his brain spinning like a dervish on Ecstasy . . .

although he probably wouldn't have phrased it to her in those terms. How would he phrase it, though? He'd never been good at playing the suave romantic. Diane's reconciliation with Sal was all the proof he needed of *that*. She would rather be with a witless tub of goo—a filthy, murdering Mafioso— just because Sal had written her that idiotic letter claiming she made him want to be "a better man," like "that fat old guy" in *As Good as It Gets*.

Her loss, though. Fred was way past that.

"So you really aren't friends with Winnie?" Noah finally asked him. "I mean, from before you started school?"

"Friends with *Winnie*?" Fred had to laugh. "Are you kidding? How would I even possibly get to know a guy like Winnie unless I parked cars at one of his country clubs? I've never even been to the Hamptons until today, Noah. *He's* the one who's behind this. Him and Olsen. They're sick, man. Beyond sick. Do you know that Olsen calls his own late-night Nerf basketball games in the voice of Bill Walton?"

"And films himself performing Shakespeare in drag?" Sunday added.

Noah's brow furrowed. "No. No, I didn't know that." He peered at the paper again. "Okay, so Olsen and Winnie are blackmailing people. And it looks like they've been doing this for a while. I mean, at least since freshman year." He still didn't sound completely convinced, but at least he wasn't joking around anymore. "Who else did they scam?"

Sunday handed the paper back to him. "I don't know. I haven't been able to figure out what these other initials stand for. Maybe you can."

"Maybe we should save that for later," Fred suggested. "I mean, we have other things to worry about. Like what we're going to *do*. And the possibility that Sal might be in East Hampton, looking for us."

Noah's eyes narrowed. "Sal?"

"Salvatore Viverito," Sunday whispered.

"The Beard?" Noah asked.

Sunday nodded grimly.

Fred shook his head, confused. "I don't get it. The Beard?"

"That was Sal's nickname at Wessex," Noah explained. "You know, because he was the only kid there who actually had five o'clock shadow. Most of us Wessexonians don't hit puberty until our midthirties." He cleared his throat. "But, ah, that's another story. Um . . . so, anyway, people thought Sal was a lot older than he said he was. I mean, he wasn't exactly the sharpest tool in the shed. I once heard him ask someone if *fondue* was spelled with three Os."

The Beard. The nickname filled Fred with terror. He wasn't even sure why. For one thing, Sal didn't have a beard. Anyway, Fred had seen Sal *kill* two people last night. That should have been terrifying enough. But "The Beard" . . . somehow, that made the whole Mafia connection much more real. Only guys who were in *deep*—the capos, the godfather's right-hand men, the ones who garroted people with piano wire and crushed heads in vises—only *those* guys had such benign or nonsensical nicknames.

Christ. This was bad. This was serious. Fred could just picture the episode of "Investigative Reports" . . . the way that slick, white-haired host with the melodramatic voice—Bill Kurtis or whoever—would talk about how The Beard had killed more than a hundred people, Fred Wright included. And another thing: Mafia guys with nicknames never worked alone. Nope. They all had lots of friends, and *they* all had nicknames, too. Pretty soon, Fred would be on the run from Frankie the Mustache (without the mustache) and Jimmy the Sideburns—

"Fred?" Noah asked. "Is everything all right?"

Both Sunday and Noah were staring at him. He shook his head.

"What is it?" Noah asked.

"There—there's something you should know," Fred stammered. "Sal is in the Mafia."

Noah grinned. "The Mafia, huh?"

"That's funny to you?" Fred said.

"Of course it is!" Noah exclaimed. "I gotta tell you, Fred, I always thought *my* sense of humor was whacked. But *this* . . . I don't know what to say. The timing, the delivery . . . everything. I'm a little jealous. Kudos, my man. Kudos."

Fred's eyes widened. He was flabbergasted. "Why would I joke around *now*? After everything we just told you? Do you know how crazy that is?"

Noah laughed. "Yes, Fred. Yes, I do. That's what makes it so perfect. I guess my decision to mentor you in my demented ways paid off better than I thought."

"Noah!" Sunday barked. She seized the sleeve of his jacket. "Listen to me. There's a very good chance that a Mafia hit man is trolling the streets of East Hampton right now, looking for us. Do you understand that?"

"Hey, you're wrinkling my tweed," Noah said.

Fred couldn't believe this. Noah *was* truly insane. "What's it gonna take to convince you that we're telling the truth?" he demanded.

Noah shrugged. Sunday let go of his jacket. He smoothed the rumpled fabric.

"I don't know," he said. "But that's okay. Keep on trying. It's entertaining. And it's not like I have anything else to do. I've already watched all of the Winthrops' DVDs."

By midafternoon, after several more hours of yelling and arguing and pleading (amid intermittent bouts of desperate laughter from Noah), Fred could tell that Noah was finally emerging from the heavy fog of denial. He'd stopped smiling. His face had gradually turned whiter and whiter, sort of like pasta on slow boil. He was also having a harder time keeping still. He kept getting up and sitting back down. Eventually he opted to stand in front of the bay windows and stare out at the ocean.

Fred was too tired to fidget. He and Sunday stayed slumped in the wicker couches. There wasn't much reason to look out the window, anyway. Clouds had swept in, and everything looked like dull, gray cement: the beach, the water, the sky, all of it.

"So it doesn't seem like there's a way out of this," Noah mumbled. "We're screwed."

"But there's gotta be a way out," Sunday said. "I mean, *we* haven't done anything wrong. You know? We have nothing to hide. The trick is to expose Olsen and Winnie without putting ourselves in danger, and . . . and . . ." Her voice petered out.

Fred patted her knee. He knew what she was thinking. Noah was right: They were screwed. Running away from Wessex hadn't been smart. Nope. It had been a big mistake. Because if he and Sunday hadn't run, if they'd just returned to campus from the quarry and had pretended to be completely ignorant, they would have been in better shape. Much better. Nobody would have suspected that they knew anything. Now that they were gone, Olsen and Winnie *knew* that they knew something. Which meant that by now, Sal probably did, too. Of course he did. And if that had really been Sal's car in town this morning . . .

"There's one thing I don't get, though," Noah said. "Why would Sal be after *you* guys? I mean, he just wants his money from Olsen and Winnie for the Carnegie Mansion game, right? It has nothing to do with you."

"That's not what Sal thinks," Fred said. "I'm sure he thinks the same thing *you* did—that I'm in on the scam. He thinks that I got his brother kicked out by planting tobacco on him, and that I did it on purpose, so I would be guaranteed the starting position. That way, I could throw the Carnegie Mansion game, so that Olsen could double-cross the Viveritos. He thinks that Olsen *profited* from the game, and that now he's holding out."

It was weird: Fred hadn't really put it all together himself until he'd said the whole thing out loud. And now that he had, he was very close to throwing up. He could feel his stomach rising. He closed his eyes and held his breath. It didn't help.

"But if Olsen was making so much money from gambling, why the tape and the blackmail?" Noah asked. "Why the whole Operation Time Capsule thing?"

Fred didn't answer. He couldn't. He was too queasy.

"Maybe he just wanted to make sure he had enough to cover his bets in case he lost," Sunday said. "Or maybe he just got greedy. Or maybe Winnie talked him into it. Who knows?"

The doorbell rang.

Fred's eyes popped open. *Oh, God no.*

In spite of his panic, he was struck by how the Winthrops' doorbell followed the exact same cheesy melody as the chimes at the beginning of "Someone's Knocking on the Door" by Paul McCartney's '70s schmaltz-rock band, Wings. Funny what forty-eight straight hours of sleepless horror could do to a person's mind.

"What should we do?" Sunday whispered. She glanced from Fred to Noah, then back again. "Come on! What should we do?"

"Don't ask me," Fred croaked. "If I try to talk, I'm gonna puke."

"See who it is!" Noah whispered, ducking behind their couch. "But don't answer it!"

Sunday nodded. She hurried from the living room into the front hall.

Fred clasped his hands together. *Oh, Lord God*, he prayed silently, *I'm not a religious man. You know that. I may not even necessarily believe in you that much. Wait. I didn't mean that last part. But please, please, God, spare us from the evil wrath of The Beard—*

"Jesus! Allison?"

Allison? Fred glanced back at Noah.

Sunday opened the door.

"I knew I'd find you here!" Allison shouted. The door slammed. "I knew it!"

Both Fred and Noah started smiling at the same time. *Whew.* Fred let out a shaky laugh. Life was just full of miraculous surprises, wasn't it? The idea that Fred would actually be relieved—no, *overjoyed*—to hear Allison Scott's snippy voice, to see her storm into the living room in full Bizarro Kidman form . . . well, that was almost up there with the idea that he would fall for a girl whose family decorated their East Hampton summer house with fish-shaped plaid pillows.

"Noah?" Allison spat. She glared at him. "What on earth . . . ?" She dropped a very expensive-looking piece of luggage on the floor and ground her teeth together for a moment. Then she shook her head.

"Well. This is just great. Noah Percy. The boy who disappeared. And Fred Wrong. Nice. Very nice."

"Hi, Al!" Noah said cheerily. He stopped crouching behind the couch and stood up straight. "So. What brings you to the Hamptons this time of year?"

Allison gave him a disdainful once-over. "For God's sake, Noah, put some pants on."

Noah glanced down at his scrawny legs. "You know, you're the second person in the last two weeks who's ordered me to put on pants. Is my lower half really that offensive?"

"Al, how did you find us?" Sunday asked.

Allison sighed. "It wasn't very hard, Sun. I knew you hadn't gone home to Greenwich, and you're smart enough to know that if you stayed in some cushy hotel, your parents would get the credit card receipts. Come on. You're just not that creative, original, or impulsive."

Sunday smiled flatly. "Thanks, Al. Thanks a lot."

"Oh, you know what I mean," Allison groaned. "Look, I'm tired, okay?" She flopped down in the couch across from Fred. "I was up all night, worrying to *death* over you. I had to *lie*. I hate lying. I had to sneak away from campus—without my parents' permission—and take two trains to get here. If anybody finds out, I could be suspended. I'm a little annoyed. Can't you people understand that?"

"Wait," Noah said. "Annoyed about lying, or annoyed about taking the train—"

The front door slammed again.

Fred frowned. "Is that the cleaning people?" he asked.

Sunday shook her head. "No. But I forgot to lock up after . . ." She turned toward the front hall. Her mouth fell open. She stepped back toward the bay windows.

"Well, well, well. Waddaya know?"

Fred's body went numb.

It was Sal. The Beard. Walking into Sunday's living room. Right in front of Fred. Not ten feet away. The nightmare had come true.

That *had* been Sal's Camaro this morning. He *had* come looking for them.

He didn't even seem real. He was wearing that same stupid blue nylon jogging suit, with his bushy red hair . . . only there was one difference. He was holding a gun. A pistol, to be exact. A pistol with a metallic silencer screwed onto the end of it. Fred had never seen a pistol before in real life. Or a silencer. Both looked bigger, somehow. Shinier, too. The Beard was holding a pistol with a silencer, and The Beard was probably going to use it . . . and . . . and, well—there was really pretty much just one thing left to do. Fred leaned forward and vomited onto Sunday's floor.

"Eww!" Allison cried.

Sal laughed. "That's some way of saying hello," he said. *Dat's some way uh sayin' hullo.* His accent had worsened. Or maybe Fred just hadn't remembered how bad it was.

"Hi, Salvatore," Noah said. "Remember me? I was two years below you . . . no. You don't remember. Well, that's all right. No harm done. I don't know many sophomores, myself. But one thing I do know: I hated that kid Noah Percy. Boy. That's one kid I never want to see again. Thank God he moved to Tibet, because he doesn't know a thing about organized—"

"Shut up," Sal said.

Fred stayed hunched over until he was sure he was finished throwing up. His head felt as if it were filled with gasoline. He sat up straight and gasped for air, wiping his face on his sleeve. *Oh, man.* This was shameful. Sunday had kept her cool. So had Allison. So had Noah . . . well, maybe not Noah. Fred slumped back against the fish-shaped pillows. So much for being the knight in shining armor, swooping in to save the Wessex Academy. Maybe Sal should get it over with. Maybe he should just pop a bullet into Fred and be gone.

"I wasn't sure anyone was home," Sal mused. "But when I saw Nicole Kidman Junior walk in, I knew I was in luck. This was the place where Freddy-boy had to be hiding out."

Allison's lips tightened. "What did you just call me?" she asked.

"What?" Sal said innocently. He lifted his shoulders, waving the pistol around. "Nobody ever said that you looked like Nicole Kidman before? Me and my buddy Carlton used to talk about it all the time. You were famous. I says, 'That chick looks just like Nicole Kidman.' And Carlton says, 'Yeah. She does. In a *Malice*-meets-*To Die For* kind of way.'"

"Will you please put that thing away?" Allison demanded.

"What thing?" Sal asked.

"That toy," Allison spat. She pointed at the gun.

Sal chuckled. "Oh. You mean, *this* toy?" He aimed the gun at a fish-shaped pillow at the far end of the couch Allison was sitting on, then squeezed the trigger. *Thwip!* A small cloud of white dust burst from the pillow. The explosion was very soft, very gentle. But where there had been plaid, there was nothing. The fish now had one black eye, about the size and shape of a nickel.

Fred felt his stomach rising again.

Allison's face turned greenish. "It's real," she breathed.

"You bet it is," Sal said. "So. Now that I have your attention, I'll be brief." He turned to Fred. "I tracked you down 'cause I want my money. Olsen

64

ain't gettin' me my money, so now *you* gotta get me my money. We're talking two hundred large. Two hundred thousand Gs. And another thing." *An' anudda ting.* "I want you freakin' ABs to make sure Tony gets back in and graduates. He was set up."

Fred nodded. He couldn't bring himself to look at anything but the pillow.

"Understood?" Sal asked.

Nobody replied. Fred would have liked to say yes, but he knew he'd just barf again if he opened his mouth.

Sal grinned. "You know, none of you is gettin' outta this. My family doesn't leave any loose ends. You know what happened to that fat prick Burwell and the other one, Miss Whos-its? I gave them a little 'diving lesson.' And I'm gonna give every one of *you* a diving lesson if I don't get my money. See, if I leave one witness, you'll cut a deal with the DA. The next thing I know, you're playin' Ping-Pong in some minimum-security prison for three-to-five, writin' your freakin' memoirs and screenplays about La Cosa Nostra and whatnot, and the Viveritos take the fall. And that ain't gonna happen to us. No way. You're all gonna get whacked."

Once again, the room was silent.

Fred hadn't followed one word of what Sal had said. Not that he'd really needed to. Just listening to the sound of his voice was horrifying enough.

Finally, after what seemed like several years, Noah cleared his throat. "So . . . um, what do you want us to do?" he asked. "You know, so we can avoid the whole 'getting whacked' thing."

"Hel-lo-*oo*?" Sal said. "Anybody home, genius? I want you to get me my money."

"But I don't even know what you're talking about!" Allison cried. "I have nothing to do with *any* of this!"

"You do now, Nicole," Sal said. "You got until noon Wednesday. Bring the money to my house in Quogue." He smiled. "One Stone Hill Terrace. You'll find it. It's listed in the Wessex alumni directory."

Letter to Charles Percy from Headmaster Olsen, via overnight messenger

The Honorable Headmaster Phillip Olsen
The Wessex Academy
41 South Chapel Street
New Farmington, Connecticut 06744

Mr. Charles Percy
32 Deer Run Lane
Sherman, CT 06578

October 21

Dear Charles,

Thank you for your timely reply to my letter regarding Noah's dismissal. This is indeed an extremely grave matter. I had no idea that your son hadn't returned home. I am certain, however, that he is quite well. Noah is an intelligent lad, and he would never endanger himself. As you probably know, <u>The Catcher in the Rye</u> is one of his favorite novels. Methinks he's playing Holden Caulfield, as it were—biding his time in New York City for a few days before having to deal with the humiliation of facing you. I have reason to believe that some of his friends have joined him, in fact. So I wouldn't fear for his safety.

In any event, I've given some serious thought to your "blunt" assessment of the situation, as per your previous correspondence. You were correct. So I will be equally as forthcoming. I'm not a man who has a great deal of spare time, either. As you know, the Wessex Academy is keen on building a new gym. A donation of no less than two hundred thousand dollars would allow us to do so. I would like nothing more than to readmit Noah and to ensure that the videotape he made of his own acts of depravity will never be made public.

I trust I will hear from _you_ shortly.

Yours,
The Honorable Headmaster
Phillip Olsen

Part II
The Two of Pentacles, Reversed

4

There was nothing worse than riding on a train, as far as Noah Percy could tell. You had to deal with that stale train stink, for one. It smelled like ass. Specifically, old man ass. Then there were all the cell-phone junkies, drinking light beer and eating peanuts and jabbering away and not worrying about a thing. *"Yeah, honey, we're just outside of Stamford . . . wait, I got something caught in my teeth."* And how about being jammed into a "luxury" four-person seating area? Apparently, the word *luxury* meant sitting face-to-face, like prisoners in an interrogation room. And battling your neighbor for control of the armrest. And kicking the two people across from you. While your entire butt fell asleep.

And the bathrooms stank, too.

So. There was nothing worse than riding on a train.

Okay, maybe a few things. But not many. Noah was certain of it, because he'd spent most of the last hour making a list. He'd had to do *something* to keep his mind occupied. There was no other possible diversion, except staring out the window at the passing lights. Even buses—the supposed lowest of the low, the McDonald's of human transport—even *they* provided something to stave off the boredom: they screened movies for their passengers. The Martha's Vineyard/Nantucket ferry offered free copies of *The Wall Street Journal*. And planes . . . well, he'd better not get started on planes. Moderately priced booze (not that he drank), moderately priced audiovisual entertainment (not that he ever bought the headphones), hot stewardesses (well, generally old and haggard and too heavily made-up) . . . yes, planes were paradise. Pure paradise.

Anyway, Noah had scribbled his list on the back of a receipt—the one for the eighty dollars worth of cereal and ramen noodles he'd purchased with his Visa Platinum card at the East Hampton Food Mart. He'd used very small letters, so it would all fit.

What Sucks Worse Than Riding on a Train?
The answers to what would seem like a rhetorical question
by Noah Percy

1) Returning to the school from which I was recently expelled, because I have nowhere else to go.

2) Finding a place to hide at the school. (The Waldorf, maybe? Under Hobson's bed?)
3) Being expelled for losing my virginity on film.
4) Knowing that the aforementioned film has circulated among several parties, including my friends, the Wessex administration, perhaps my parents, and probably the Mafia.
5) Knowing that if I don't come up with $200,000 by Wednesday, I'll end up taking a "diving lesson."
6) Knowing that a "diving lesson" is a euphemism for being killed by the Mafia.
7) Knowing an actual member of the Mafia.
8) The word <u>Mafia</u>.

"What are you *doing*?" Allison demanded. She kicked him.

Noah glanced up at her. Too bad Sunday hadn't taken the seat directly across from him. Oh, well. At least the train drowned out the constant grinding of Allison's teeth.

"I'm writing a screenplay about La Cosa Nostra," he said.

Allison scowled. "There's nothing funny about this, you know."

"I didn't say there was. I wish Hobson were here. He could do a little rap for us. *'Yo, girl, I got a bad case of scrofula. Even worse, I got problems wit' da Mafia—'"*

"Shut up!" Allison barked.

"I'm sorry," Noah said.

"Really, Noah," Sunday said. "Shut up."

"What? I'm just using humor as a defense mechanism, the way you do. Also, if you say the word *Mafia* enough times, it'll start to sound like gibberish. You know how that happens? Try it. Pick a word. Like *scrofula*. Then say it a bunch of times, over and over and over—"

"Shut up!" Fred barked.

Noah looked back down at his list. He was just trying to help, for Pete's sake.

"Listen, you guys," Sunday whispered. "We're gonna be in New Farmington in less than an hour. We have to start coming up with a plan."

Allison raised her eyebrows. "A plan? Excuse me? I don't know about *you*, but my plan is to go straight to Headmaster Olsen and report all of this. I won't have an alumnus march into my friend's home and fire a pistol into her furniture."

Everybody stared at her.

Noah had to admit he was pretty impressed. The magnificent Allison Scott. It was more difficult to instill the fear of the Mob in her than it was to offend her sense of decorum. He wished *he* were that deranged. It would be a hell of a lot better than running his mouth like an idiot in a useless effort to forget how terrified he was.

"What?" Allison said defensively. "You don't actually believe that Headmaster Olsen could have anything to do with this, do you?"

"Not *this* again," Fred groaned.

"Allison, I don't really care *what* you believe," Sunday stated. "But for better or worse, we're in this together. And I'm willing to forgive a lot of the crap—"

"Sunday, you're being incredibly unfair," Allison said. "You know—"

"Just let me finish," Sunday interrupted, gently but firmly. "If you go to Olsen, I guarantee you that some of us won't survive. Think about that. Think about what it really means. Mr. Burwell and Miss Burke are *dead*. Do you understand that? *Dead.* And think about another thing: If Sal was able to track me down at my summer house, how hard do you think it would be for him to track *you* down? Or your parents? Or anyone else he could possibly threaten?"

Allison blinked at her. "You're sure Mr. Burwell and Miss Burke are dead?"

"Unless they survived falling into the quarry," Sunday said.

"I don't believe this," Allison murmured to herself. She squirmed in her seat. "I should never have come looking for you. I just wanted a cell phone. That's all."

Noah was puzzled. "A cell phone?"

"Yeah. I saw that Winnie had one, and he said he got it because Olsen put him on a special committee, and *I* want to be on that committee, and Winnie keeps getting calls from somebody named Sal—" Allison stopped abruptly. Her eyes widened. "Oh my God. *Sal.* Sal! Sal Viverito!" Her lips began to tremble. "It *is* true! That's why Winnie's been acting so weird. Sal wants money from Winnie, too. . . ."

Allison stared right at Noah, as if she were expecting him to respond. He had no idea what she was talking about. It seemed to be the theme of the evening: a total breakdown of communication. But as long as she finally believed them, that was fine by him.

"So what are we going to do?" she wailed.

"Shh," Sunday whispered. She poked her head into the aisle and glanced around the train car. "That's what we have to figure out, okay? Just relax."

Noah nodded. "Right. We have to relax and figure out a way to outsmart Winslow Ellis, Headmaster Olsen, and the Mafia." He smiled, crumpling the list in his hand. He felt as if his stomach had been ripped from his body and placed on his seat's folding tray. "No problem."

"You know, there is a way we can do it," Fred said.

"Of course there is," Noah said.

"I'm being serious," Fred said. He leaned forward and lowered his voice. "Think about it. The key to this whole thing is greed. You saw the Operation Time Capsule breakdown. Winnie and Olsen are the two greediest bastards on the planet. And I bet hands down that they're more loyal to money than they are to each other."

Allison frowned. "Winnie's not *so* greedy," she said.

Fred glared at her.

She lowered her eyes. "Okay. So what if they're greedy? What does *that* mean?"

"It means they have a weakness. Now. The first step to beating somebody is finding their weakness. I mean, this is going to sound weird, but we should think of it like a game of basketball. The only way to beat somebody better than you is to find a weakness and exploit it." Fred paused for a minute and glanced at Noah, as if for confirmation.

Noah blinked. Maybe this was some sort of manly thing he should know about. But the truth was, he hated basketball. He liked Frisbee, though. "Right," he said.

"We also need to think about exactly what *we* need to accomplish. And the way I see it, we need to accomplish three things. Tell me if I'm wrong." Fred started counting off on his fingers. "One: We need to get two hundred thousand dollars, at least for the time being. Two: We need to expose Winnie and Olsen to the public. Three: We need to stay in school and graduate."

Nobody said a word.

Noah glanced at Sunday and Allison. He had no clue what they were thinking. All he knew was that number three was out of the question for him, because he'd already been expelled. He cleared his throat. "I can think of a couple other things we need to accomplish, Fred," he said. "Like staying alive, maybe?"

Fred leaned back in his chair. "The key to staying alive is to get Sal his money," he said.

"Which brings us back to the first problem," Sunday said. "How on earth are *we* possibly going to come up with two hundred thousand dollars? Do you know how hard that is?"

"Actually . . . um, I have some experience with this," Noah said. "And I can vouch for the fact that, yes, it *is* hard. I once tried to make two hundred thousand dollars—fairly recently, in fact—and I ended up losing four thousand instead. And crashing the school's Internet server. And getting kicked out. But, you know, that's a story for another time." He shrugged.

"Well, don't worry," Fred said. "I know how to do it. *And* get you back in school."

"How?" Noah, Sunday, and Allison asked at the same time.

"We turn Winnie and Olsen against each other," Fred said. "*We* start doing the blackmailing. We convince Winnie that Olsen is panicking about getting caught—which I'm sure he is, anyway—and that he's trying to save himself by screwing Winnie in some way. We convince Winnie that only *we* can stop Olsen from doing it. But the price has to be right."

Noah frowned. That sounded like the dumbest thing he'd ever heard. It didn't make any sense.

On the other hand, he supposed he should be relieved that *somebody* had a plan. But he wasn't. And he didn't see himself getting relief any time soon.

Letter from Charles Percy to Phillip Olsen, via overnight messenger

Mr. Charles Percy
32 Deer Run Lane
Sherman, CT 06578

Phillip Olsen
The Wessex Academy
41 South Chapel Street
New Farmington, Connecticut 06744

October 22

Phil:

I know that you don't expect me to write you a two hundred thousand dollar check. You're smarter than that. You know that I can pick up the phone right now, call Carnegie Mansion, and have Noah admitted there for the remainder of the year. It doesn't matter what you have on tape. You could have a video of Noah chopping small children to bits, and CM would still take him.

CM knows I've got the money to build ten big bucks gyms. They'd just love to get a piece of me, particularly at your expense. So ask yourself: How would that look, after three generations of Percys? People see what they want to see. You're a fund-raiser, so you know that. If the Percys decide to sever ties with Wessex over these silly threats of yours—which I intend to make public—I guarantee you'll have a lot of unhappy trustees and parents. They'll side with me, Phil. Your endowment will go south like a duck in winter. Meanwhile, Noah will successfully graduate from one of the most prestigious boarding schools in the country—that being your big bucks arch rival.

So here's your answer: I'm paying you nothing. Now find my son and get him back in class, or I'll publish these letters and bring you up on charges of negligence and attempted blackmail.

Yours,
Charles Percy

From: Undisclosed Sender
To: Undisclosed Recipient
Subject: Last resort

FW, SW, and AS are back. I haven't been able
to get to them yet. NP, apparently, is still
missing. I heard from his father this
morning. He won't pay. I am genuinely
concerned. I've decided to take drastic
action to ensure both that Sal is paid
immediately and that we temporarily distract
the campus from the missing PBs.

From: Undisclosed Sender
To: Undisclosed Recipient
Subject: re: Last resort

I'm concerned, too. What sort of drastic
action are you talking about?

From: Undisclosed Sender
To: Undisclosed Recipient
Subject: re: re: Last resort

I've decided to "kidnap" MW. I'll fill you
in on the details later. I'm certain her
family will pay the ransom. She's an only
child. Once we have the money, we can pin
the crime on the PBs. We'll furnish
evidence to prove that they killed each
other in a squabble over the ransom—and
that knowledge of the money's whereabouts
died with them. In all likelihood, we'll

have to dispose of MW, as well. I've given
this a great deal of thought. I don't see
any other way to solve all our problems in
one decisive move. Delete this message
immediately.

Mackenzie hadn't wanted it to come to the tarot cards. She really hadn't.

They were a last resort. For emergency use only. Really never to be touched, or even *looked* at. Yet here she was, alone in the triple, staring right at the deck, wrapped in its protective silk shroud on the Sven Larsen table. (Or maybe the cards were on the bench and *she* was on the table; she could never remember which was which.)

You have to do a reading. You know you do.

It was true. Allison and Sunday had left her no other choice. They hadn't said a single word since mysteriously returning last night, just before check-in. Not a *peep*. Not even a "good night." After everything! They'd just gone straight to bed. And this morning, they'd run off to breakfast before Mackenzie could even get dressed. . . . It was crazy. She still hadn't the faintest clue where Sunday had been, or how Allison had found Sunday, or why everyone on campus was freaking out because Mr. Burwell and Miss Burke had run off together (that was one of the rumors, anyway, not that Mackenzie believed it). . . . No, it was beyond crazy. It was too much. Whatever was going on, she knew that Allison and Sunday knew. They *had* to know.

So why wouldn't they just *tell* her?

All right, she could guess why. They were trying to protect her. The less she knew, the safer she was. But she didn't care about herself. She cared about *them*. She'd spent all yesterday alone, worrying her head off. (Although technically, she hadn't really been alone; she'd been with Hobson, but they hadn't been *doing* anything, because he was just trying to console her—and that didn't matter.) No, all that mattered were Allison and Sunday. They were in real danger now. Life-threatening danger. Mackenzie was certain of it. Being born under a Pisces moon had its benefits.

Still, those benefits only went so far. That was the whole problem. Her natural psychic ability could give her a *hunch*. Numerology and astrology could sharpen the hunch, point her in the right direction—but when it came to specifics, she needed something more. If she was going to help her friends, she needed to know *exactly* what was going on. And if they insisted on giving her the silent treatment . . .

Right. She took a deep breath. She'd said it to herself a thousand times in the past few weeks: Desperate times called for desperate measures. And times had never been more desperate. She stared at the cards. Her heart pounded. The white silk glittered in the Monday morning sun.

"Don't be scared," she whispered.

But she *was* scared. She was scared of the tarot's power. Because the only time she'd ever used them—

Man, oh man.

Mackenzie shivered. She hadn't thought about this in a long, long time.

It had all started on a trip to New York City. Just her and Sunday. It was the summer before freshman year. At Mackenzie's insistence, they'd stopped at a fortune-teller in Greenwich Village. It was a tiny little place below the sidewalk; you had to walk down a little stairwell to get to it, and it was barely visible from the street—just a neon light in a window: PALM READINGS, FIVE DOLLARS. Yet somehow, Mackenzie had been drawn to it. Maybe it was that psychic intuition. Or maybe she was just tired of shopping for shoes. Whatever the reason, they'd gone inside, and Sunday told her to go first, and . . . well, that was when it had gotten weird.

The fortune-teller was this sketchy old lady with hairs on her chin. And these big black eyes. That was what Mackenzie remembered the most: the eyes, like onyx. Her name was Maurice. No . . . Maura. Or Moe. Something like that. Anyway, she sat behind a little table with a crystal ball in a tiny room lit by candles—the decor was actually pretty cool, now that Mackenzie thought about it—and she just *stared* at Mackenzie for about five minutes. At least it felt like five minutes. And then she told Mackenzie that she couldn't give her a reading.

"You have no need of my services," Moe said. "But please accept these as a gift, for twenty dollars."

Mackenzie didn't get it. She was actually a little offended. But then Moe handed over a pack of tarot cards—*this* pack of tarot cards—and told Mackenzie that she was perfectly capable of telling her own fortunes. Moe could see that Mackenzie was "blessed." The whole thing was just too freaky. Mackenzie handed over a fifty by accident, then bolted.

And that wasn't even the worst of it.

No . . . when Mackenzie got home that night, she took the cards out of her purse and decided to give herself a reading. She asked the cards about her love life.

And that was when *it* happened. *IT.*

The tarot revealed to her that she would secretly kiss the boy of her dreams that year, that the boy would become involved with one of her best friends . . . and that four years later, she and the boy would be reunited.

And it had all come true.

Until now, Mackenzie hadn't once considered the *hugeness* of it. She couldn't. She'd deliberately forgotten about the whole thing, in fact. There was even a psychological term for that kind of forgetfulness: *repression.* Yup. For four long years, she'd repressed the memory that she and Hobson were destined to be together. And she'd known it all along, subconsciously. Only once had the tarot's message occurred to her—that day in the Value City Appliance Warehouse, a couple of weeks ago—but even then, she'd shut it out of her mind. She couldn't deal with it. How could a person possibly deal with something like that? Hooking up with Hobson wasn't like predicting the score of a basketball game, or knowing that a certain flight would be canceled. It meant alienating one of her best friends. It meant forming a mystical union. It was no accident that she and Hobson had been together in past lives as Janis Joplin and Pig

Pen. Their romantic destiny was sewn into the fabric of the cosmos. . . .

But this wasn't about him. No. It was about Sunday and Allison. What was done was done. So there was no point in procrastinating any longer.

With trembling fingers, Mackenzie unwrapped the silk covering and shuffled the deck. She just had to keep reminding herself that there was no reason to be scared of her own gift. She should embrace it. She should *harness* it. For the sake of her friends. All of them. Not just her roommates. Noah, too. Even Fred. Janis herself sang: *"Try to help your brother, if you can."*

After about a minute of shuffling, Mackenzie set the deck back on the table.

Now, which method of divination should she use—the Ancient Celtic or Tree of Life? Well, actually she didn't really know how to use either, so it was probably best just to use the Mackenzie Wilde method, which was to ask a question, then pick three cards.

She laid her fingers on the deck, then hesitated. Before she dove into this, she should probably just do a sample reading for herself—just to get the ball rolling and the forces of the universe warmed up. Sure. Why not? Then she would do readings for Sunday, Allison, Noah, and Fred. Hobson, she would save for last. She held her breath and closed her eyes, clearing her mind of all but one thought:

What's going to happen to me today?

With that, she turned the card over.

It was key 4 of the major arcana: the Emperor. It was upside down.

Mackenzie stared down at the image of the mean-looking king, sitting on the throne with a scepter in his hand. He sort of looked like Olsen, except with hair. And a crown and a beard, too. Now that she remembered it, a reversed Emperor was pretty bad news. For one thing, it symbolized that you were emotionally immature and overly dependent on your parents (no need to overanalyze that one), but it also indicated that some evil force was lurking in the background, waiting to do harm or to try to steal money from you or your family.

So it wasn't looking like this particular day was going to be one of her best. It was probably going to be pretty lousy. Oh, well. She placed the card faceup next to the deck, then drew another.

This one was the Tower—key 16 of the major arcana. It was also upside down. Mackenzie swallowed. *Uh-oh.* A reversed Tower was even worse than a reversed Emperor. The image was really creepy, too, with lightning hitting the medieval-style minaret and the guy falling out of the window at the top. . . . She was starting to remember why she was scared of the cards. A reversed Tower usually meant that you were going to be locked up. Imprisoned. Maybe not literally, but definitely symbolically.

She dropped the card on top of the Emperor.

So today wasn't just going to be lousy; it was going to *suck*. Whatever. She just had to stay calm. There was no reason to freak out. Not yet, anyway.

Card number three was . . .

The Two of Pentacles, reversed.

Finally. Mackenzie exhaled. This wasn't so bad. At least it was part of the minor arcana, which meant that it wasn't as powerful as the other two cards. Generally, a reversed Two of Pentacles meant that you were pretending to be happy when you weren't (no argument there), and that letters or messages were being exchanged among—

"Psst," somebody whispered outside the door. "Yo, Mack? You in there?"

She whirled around. "Hobson?"

"Yeah. Can you open up?"

Mackenzie ran to the door and unlocked it. "Hey," she whispered. She glanced out into the hall. "Are you okay?"

Hobson shrugged. "Maintaining, yo. Wassup, girl?"

"Uh . . . nothing," she mumbled. As usual, she turned bright red. She really had to stop doing that.

And she *would*, just as soon as Hobson stopped dressing up in these ridiculously sexy clothes. It wasn't fair. It was as if he were *trying* to make her blush. He was wearing a pair of extra-baggy khakis, which hung perfectly on his butt, and that Sean John sweatshirt she loved, and a backward blue baseball hat that heightened the blue in his eyes and pushed his blond hair down in these cute little bangs. . . . *Oh, brother. Enough already.* "So what are you doing here?" she asked. "I mean, not that I'm bummed. I'm actually really psyched. . . ." She closed her mouth. Better to quit while she was ahead.

"I saw you weren't at breakfast," Hobson said casually. "So I decided to come check on you. You know, just to make sure you were all right. What with all the craziness."

Mackenzie nodded. "Here, come in." She grabbed his hand and tugged him into the triple, then closed the door. "Has anybody seen Mr. Burwell and Miss Burke yet?"

Hobson shook his head. "Nah. But that reminds me. I saw Olsen when I was coming out of the dining hall. He's looking for you. He said it's urgent."

"Olsen's looking for *me*?" Mackenzie whispered. All of a sudden, she felt very uneasy. She let go of Hobson's hand. "Are you sure?"

"Yeah," Hobson replied. He swung his backpack

off his shoulder and dropped it on the floor. His eyes flashed to the table. A grin spread across his face. "Damn, yo! You messin' with tarot cards? Baby, you just keep takin' freakiness to the next *level*! I thought—"

"Oh, my God!" Mackenzie shrieked. In that instant, it all came together—*BAM!*—and the tarot's message became crystal clear. *Of course!* The horrible realization was like the bolt of lightning on the Tower card. "Hobson, Olsen wants to kidnap me!"

Hobson blinked. "Uh . . . what?"

Mackenzie stared at him, wide-eyed. She nodded violently. "That's what the reading means! Olsen wants to hold me for ransom!"

"The . . . reading?"

"Here, come look." She dragged him over to the table and pointed at the cards. "See? Every card I picked was a reverse! You know, upside down!"

"Maybe the deck's upside down, yo," Hobson said.

Mackenzie shook her head. "No. It can't be upside down. See, the tarot is supposed to represent the hidden store of all wisdom and knowledge in the universe. And there is no upside down or right side up in the universe. Everything is one."

Hobson seemed concerned. "Mack, you're buggin' again," he said.

"No, no, no. I'm serious. The Emperor means that I'm in danger. The Tower means that I'm going to be imprisoned. And the Two of Pentacles means that messages are going to be sent—you know, like ransom notes and stuff." She spoke in such a rush that she could barely get all the words out. "Anyway, just *look* at the Emperor. He looks like Olsen, doesn't he?"

Hobson raised his eyebrows. He stared at the card for a few seconds. "I don't know, Mack," he said quietly. "I don't see a bow tie. And I don't see a wack comb-over, either. This dude is kinda fresh, yo. Check the robes and the beard. Olsen doesn't have a beard, right?"

"You really don't believe me?" Mackenzie asked in a shaky voice.

"It's not that." Hobson took her hands and looked her in the eye. "I just think we gotta be careful, you know? Make sure our imaginations don't get the best of us."

"But Olsen is capable of *anything*," Mackenzie pointed out. "I mean, think about it. We know he dresses in drag, that he set up your brother for a pot bust and tried to blackmail your family for it, that he places bets against his own basketball team with the Mafia. . . . I mean, the list goes on and on. Kidnapping would be *nothing* to Olsen."

Hobson was silent. "I see what you mean," he said finally.

Mackenzie took a deep breath. She drew Hobson closer to her, so that their faces were only inches apart. "That's not all," she whispered. "See . . . I *know* the cards always tell the truth. I'm positive of it."

"You are? How?"

"Because they told me once that you and I were meant to be together," she said.

Hobson leaned forward and kissed her gently on the lips. "Okay, Mack," he said. "Okay. Just chill. Let's just hang here for a bit and figure something out."

But Mackenzie's mind was already racing. "No. We gotta get to Olsen before he gets to me," she said. "Come on. I think I know exactly what to do."

Within ten minutes of leaving Reed Hall, a total of *four* people stopped Mackenzie and Hobson on the path, and all of them said the exact same thing.

"Oh, hi, Mackenzie—did you know that Olsen is looking for you?"

First it was Hadley Bryant. Then Boyce Sutton. Then Carter Boyce. Then Kate Ramsey. If this wasn't evidence of a kidnapping plot, Mackenzie didn't know *what* was. Even Hobson was beginning to get freaked. He'd actually started holding her hand. In *public,* even though they weren't officially going out or anything. His palm was clammy. The rumors were bound to start flying about the two of them, if they hadn't already. It was a good thing that so few people were out and about: most were in first period, or if they had first period free, they were in their dorms. Mackenzie had French Conversation, but she didn't care. Not anymore. Because for the second time this month, she was going to skip a class for a noble cause. She was going to bring down Olsen once and for all.

"Yo, I don't know about this, Mack," Hobson muttered. He ducked low as they veered off the path, tiptoeing through the shrubbery toward the white picket fence in back of Olsen's mansion. "You sure busting into Olsen's crib is such a hot idea?"

"Definitely. Now's our best chance. I mean, think about it. It's *his* house. This is the last place he'd look for me." She hesitated, peering into the kitchen windows. "Besides, Fred and Sunday break in here all the time."

Hobson stared at her. "They do?"

"Come on," she whispered.

She scrambled over the fence, nearly falling flat on her face, and ran to the back door. She turned the latch. Just as she'd suspected, it was open. Her heart lurched. *This is it!* She glanced back at Hobson. He tossed his backpack over the fence first, then climbed over it as carefully as possible, so as not to dirty his sweatshirt. After taking a second to dust off his pants, he picked up his backpack and strolled calmly across the lawn. He slouched as he went, with his hands in his pockets, bobbing his head in time to some silent beat. Maybe he thought that would make him look less suspicious.

"Hurry up!" Mackenzie hissed.

She closed the door behind him, then grabbed his hand and dragged him through the living room and around the corner to the narrow hall that led to the cellar. How crazy was this? Sneaking around Olsen's mansion when she should have been in first period! Her heart was beating so fast she could barely breathe. But amazingly, she wasn't really all that scared. She almost felt as if she were in some altered state of consciousness. Like she was walking on hot coals. Or in a trance. Or maybe just drunk. Then again, the last time she'd been here, she *had* been drunk—at the Student Council Dinner. Yet, for some reason, she was also consumed by a vivid fantasy of grabbing Hobson right now and making out with him passionately.

"What is your problem?" she whispered out loud. She plunged down the stairwell to Olsen's cellar. "Focus!"

"Hocus Pocus," Hobson said behind her.

She glanced over her shoulder. "What?"

He chuckled. "Nothing. Just freestylin', yo. I love the way you talk to yourself."

Mackenzie grinned. "Really?"

"Yeah. It's mad . . . holy moly."

The two of them stopped at the bottom of the stairs. Mackenzie's jaw dropped.

"Holy moly" was right.

The cellar was even more frightening than she'd imagined. Even *after* what Sunday had told her. There was the "World's Sexiest Bachelor" newspaper article, obviously—but that wasn't the worst of it. The walls were *covered* with fake articles. And the basketball court was easily forty feet across, with nets at either end and markings on the floor, just like in the gym. How much money had Olsen spent to build it? But the trophy case—that was what was really freaking her out. It was full of brass goblets and little statues, and every one of them had to be phony. . . . There was also what looked like a small-scale version of a pirate's treasure chest near the bottom. And a basketball uniform with Olsen's name on it. His number was 27. *That* figured. Mackenzie turned to Hobson. "Can you believe this?" she whispered.

Hobson shrugged. He glanced around the room, then nodded, as if impressed. "Your son made it, Mama," he said with a Cuban accent. "He's a success."

Mackenzie frowned at him. Now was not exactly

the most appropriate time to be joking around and quoting *Scarface*. They were in a madman's basement, for God's sake. She was in danger of being kidnapped. But the next thing she knew, she was giggling. So was he. The giggles turned to laughter. Suddenly they were both cackling hysterically.

"Shut up!" Mackenzie whispered.

Hobson clamped his hand over his mouth. He didn't stop, though.

"We have work to do, okay?" She tried to sound serious, but she just ended up laughing harder. She shook her head and marched over to the trophy case. Now, if *she* were a Capricorn with Capricorn rising, she would probably keep the documents and videotapes of all her evil deeds locked up in here somewhere. (Capricorns often masked their true intentions with self-congratulatory behavior.) Sunday had mentioned that she'd found that Shakespeare tape in the chest upstairs, but Olsen wouldn't make the same mistake twice. He was a smart guy. He was also a control freak. All Capricorns were. Especially the criminals.

"Watcha lookin' at?" Hobson asked.

Mackenzie scanned the glass door for a latch. "I'm just trying to see if . . ." *There.* Right at the bottom, there was a little metal lever. She clicked it, and the door swung open.

Hobson walked up beside her. "Yo, dawg, you

wanna swipe one of these trophies?" he asked. He was grinning. He looked so cute, like a little kid who'd just been let loose in FAO Schwarz at Christmastime. "Or how about this, yo?" He grabbed the uniform's jersey off its hooks and held it up against his body, modeling it for her. "Whaddya think? Am I the world's sexiest bachelor or what?"

"Definitely," she said. She glanced at the shelves again. Actually, maybe Hobson was on to something here. If they took Olsen's uniform and some of these fake awards, that might be enough to scare him into—

"Oh, my God," Hobson gasped. The jersey slipped from his fingers and fell to the floor. "Mack, check it out! That's my brother!"

He pointed at a trophy on the top shelf, the middle in a series of three. All three were identical— smaller and less gaudy than the others. The design was simple: just a brass statue of a stopwatch mounted on a thick mahogany base that was about eight inches on a side. Mackenzie stood on her tiptoes and squinted at the inscription next to Hobson's shaky finger.

O.T.C. 1999
WALKER CROWE

"What's 'O.T.C.'?" she whispered.
"I don't know. Check out these others, though.

Nineteen ninety-eight, Grady Thomas. I remember that dude . . . and in two thousand, Montgomery Richard. Damn!" Hobson glanced at Mackenzie. He wasn't smiling anymore. "Do you think that these have got something to do with how Olsen tried to blackmail Walker? I mean, it just seems *weird*, right? Walker didn't even play sports. Montgomery didn't, either. That dude must've smoked two cartons a *week,* yo. Homeboy was *always* kickin' it at the Waldorf. Why would Walker and Montgomery and Grady get trophies? And why would Olsen have them?"

Mackenzie shook her head. All at once, she was very scared. Hobson was right: it *did* seem weird. Much too weird for her liking, in fact. She was suddenly very conscious of the fact that they'd been puttering around in Olsen's cellar for several minutes now. Maybe coming here wasn't so smart after all. Maybe it was stupid. It certainly wouldn't be the first time she'd done something stupid in her life.

"I'm takin' these," Hobson muttered. He wriggled out of his backpack straps and ripped the bag open, then started shoving all the O.T.C. trophies inside it—along with the basketball uniform. "If this has got Walker's name on it, it belongs to *him*." He hesitated for another second, then grabbed the treasure chest and tucked that under his arm.

"Hobson, maybe we should go now," Mackenzie said.

"Word." He slung the bag over his shoulder and slammed the glass door. The remaining trophies rattled. "We're out. Let's go to my crib."

It wasn't until they were just outside Hobson's room—safely inside Logan Hall—that Mackenzie was finally able to relax enough to speak.

"Why'd you take that chest?" she asked, still struggling to catch her breath.

Hobson shrugged. He fumbled with his key. "My shelf isn't big enough for all my CDs," he said. "And I thought . . ." He frowned at the lock.

"What is it?"

"Nothing," Hobson said. He sniffed. His nose wrinkled. "You smell that? It smells like some-body's cooking up noodles."

He pushed the door open.

Mackenzie nearly fainted.

Noah Percy was sitting on Hobson's bed.

She blinked, to make sure she wasn't dreaming. She wasn't. He was right smack in the middle of the leopard-skin comforter, in Hobson's bathrobe, framed by an Olde English 800 poster on one side and a Jay-Z poster on the other. A steaming plastic bowl of ramen noodles sat in his lap. A notebook and pencil lay beside him. He was just . . . *there*, chowing down, writing something, as if it were the most natural thing in the world that he should be in Hobson's room—and not home, or at public school, or in an insane asylum, or wherever somebody went after they were booted out of Wessex.

"Noah?" Mackenzie breathed.

He stared at them for a second. One of the noodles dangled from his lips.

"Howdy," he said.

Noah's note intended for Hobson

Hobson!

What's up, homeboy? What's the dilly-o? Word to your Moms.

So. I really need to ask you a favor. Can I stay in your room for a while? See, I can't really go home. Well, actually it's more like I don't want to. I can't face my dad. I got issues, homes. Not that this is news to you or anything. But, yo, I'll let you in on a little secret. Peep this: Sunday and Fred Wright plan on bringing down Olsen and Winnie.

You do know what's going on with Olsen and Winnie, don't you?

They're ill, G. They were the ones who filmed Miss Burke and me. Now if that's not wack, I don't know what is. So Sunday and Fred are going to help me get them back. (Unfortunately, we have to raise 200 large to pay off the Mob first, but that's another story.) I don't know what the exact plan is, but it's going to involve some kind of fake letter. Even Allison's in on it. Can you believe it? Homegirl is actually going to kick it James Bond style! She feels personally betrayed because Winnie and Headmaster Olsen compromised everything the Wessex Academy stands for. (Her words, not mine.) I've never seen her so pissed.

They might have already gotten to him. Olsen is seriously

bugging. I just saw him out the window, and he was running up and down the path—this way and that, all frazzled—stopping every single student to ask them something.

This whole thing is mad crazy, yo. <u>Mad</u> crazy.

You have to keep all this on the DL, but if you want to hear more, you might want to let me stay in your room. Plus, not to get all technical, but you still owe me from that time in sixth grade when I let you hide out at my crib after you broke the windshield of your dad's Porsche.

Your homey,
Noah

P.S. Have you heard the new Wu-Tang record? It has a killer sample from the Isley Brothers. I'd find that Isley Brothers album if I were you, homeslice. For the ladies. You know what I'm saying.

6

"I don't know about this," Sunday said. "Are you really sure this is going to work?"

"No," Fred said. "But if it doesn't, we're screwed."

Sunday nodded. *Right.* She could have supplied that answer herself. She sat down on Fred's bed and stared at his silhouette as he typed the last few words: *clackety-clack-clack.* How could he even see what he was doing? Aside from the pale blue glow of the computer screen, the room was nearly pitch black. Fred had hung a towel over his window—a makeshift curtain, as rooms in Ellis didn't have curtains—because he didn't want to be spotted from the path outside in case anybody was looking for them (it *was* lunchtime, and neither of them had gone to any classes) . . . although, of course, the towel must have looked extremely suspicious.

And if Olsen suspected that they *were* holed up in here, he could just open Fred's door with a master key.

Not that Sunday was worried about getting caught or anything.

Actually, she wasn't. No, right now, for better or worse, she was more worried about wording this letter properly. Olsen had a specific tone that was extremely difficult to mimic, if only because it was so demented. She'd already tried it herself, and after about a thousand drafts, she'd only come up with this:

Date: October 22
From: Headmaster Olsen
To: Pearson Ellis
Re: Winslow Ellis

Dear Mr. Ellis,

As you know, I've always held your son in the highest esteem. It pains me to have to inform you of his involvement in various illegal and immoral moneymaking schemes on the Wessex campus. Details attached.

Winslow is at a critical juncture in his education and cannot afford any blemishes on his record. Toward that end, I am offering to overlook his transgressions in exchange for a donation of $300,000 to the enclosed account number.

I trust you will take care of this matter in a timely fashion.

> Yours truly,
> Phillip Olsen
> Headmaster

It wasn't nearly convincing enough. Besides, if anybody could tell a forgery, Winnie could. The fact that they were using the personal stationery they'd stolen from Olsen would help, yes. But Winnie would already be in an apprehensive frame of mind. Not to mention the fact that $300,000 was a bit steep.

"Done," Fred said. He took a deep breath and pushed back from his desk. The folding chair squeaked on the floor.

Sunday stood again. Her legs trembled. "Can I read it before you print it out?"

"Yeah, of course," Fred said. "I hope it's all right. I mean, you know Olsen way better than I do."

"I do?" she murmured. "I don't know if anybody

knows him. Anyway, you've got a way with words. I'm sure you did a great job." She leaned over him and gently massaged his bony shoulders as she peered at the screen. "Forging letters from the headmaster should be a piece of cake for a juvenile delinquent like you."

Mr. Pearson Ellis
4 Oneida Drive
Greenwich, CT 06175

October 22

Dear Pearson,

I wish that I could be writing to you under happier circumstances. In the words of the Bard: "That before you, and next unto high heaven, I love your son!" So it is with the utmost pain and regret that I must inform you that I have decided to expel Winslow.

My reasons are as follows:

A year ago, nearly to the day, Winslow was investigated by the Securities Exchange Commission for running a nefarious enterprise from the grounds of the Wessex Academy. Much to our collective dismay, these charges proved true. In light of Winslow's promises to live up to the Ellis name—a name borne by so many of the campus buildings—and out of respect for our long-standing personal relationship, I forgave these transgressions with the understanding that such behavior would never be repeated.

In recent days, however, it has come to my attention that Winslow has broken his promise. The evidence is incontrovertible. Enclosed are the incriminating documents and videotapes. As you will see, the list of his most recent crimes includes racketeering, gambling, and perhaps even murder. And as hard as it may be to believe, it also appears that Winnie has forged ties with members of organized crime to profit from the plethora of his illegal activities.

I would like to assure you that these materials are secure. I am the only one who has seen them, and I have no intention of releasing them to the authorities until we have spoken. I pray that Winnie will mend his ways and use his enormous potential to transform himself into the productive member of society we both know him to be.

Yours,
The Honorable Phillip Olsen

P.S. The science building you so generously donated is officially under construction! As of today, the foundation has been laid. We were hoping to add a state-of-the-art planetarium, as well. The contractors inform me that the cost will be in the $200,000.00 range.

Sunday's hands slipped from his shoulders. "I don't believe it," she said.

"That bad, huh?"

"Bad? Are you *nuts*? Fred, this is—I-I—it's incredible," she stammered.

He glanced up at her. "Really?" He didn't sound very convinced.

"Fred, you're a genius. I'm not exaggerating. This sounds more like Olsen than Olsen sounds like himself. I mean, the P.S. bit is the most brilliant thing I've ever read. And where did you get that Shakespeare quote?"

He shrugged. "*All's Well that Ends Well.*" He turned back to the screen. "It's the only Shakespeare play I know. It was Diane's favorite. She forced me to go see it twice when it was playing at the Shakespeare Rep in D.C." He laughed bitterly. "At least she was good for something, huh?"

At the mention of Diane's name, Sunday felt a

sudden flash of jealousy. Then she rolled her eyes. *What is my problem?* Fred was *over* Diane. And even if he wasn't (which he was), he had every right to have some leftover feelings for her, because he and Sunday still weren't officially going out (although they spent every single second together) . . . actually, that wasn't the problem at all.

No. Sunday knew exactly what the problem was. Her problem was that her libido had gone haywire again—this time, as a result of watching Fred write a phony letter, an activity that was as sexy as, say, picking one's nose. It was sick. Sick, but true. She felt an overwhelming compulsion to throw herself at the guy. Because of a good forgery.

Okay, maybe that was a slight understatement. Compared to her lame attempt, his creation was a work of art.

"So you really think it's okay?" he asked.

Sunday sighed. "Let me put it this way, Fred. It's not going to get any better." She reached over and pulled the towel off the window, then tossed it on the bed. The sunlight made her squint. "Come on. We should go. We've been in here too long. We've got to find Winnie."

"He's at the Waldorf or Marriott," Fred said.

"How do you know?"

"He always hits the smoking spots around lunchtime.

Those are the peak sales hours." Fred paused. "But what should we do about Olsen's signature? It won't look real without it."

Sunday chewed her thumbnail. "I was thinking about that," she mumbled. "Go ahead and print it out. I'll handle the signature."

Fred looked at her. "You sure?"

"Yeah, I'm sure," she said. She absently tucked a couple of stray hairs behind her ear. *Blecch.* They felt like straw. All this sneaking around and cloak-and-dagger stuff was taking a serious toll on her personal hygiene. If they ever survived this insanity, she would book a spa weekend in Saratoga first thing. She deserved one, for God's sake—Saturday classes be damned. "I know Olsen's signature pretty well," she added. "I've grown up with it. He's been writing to me since I was a baby."

"Writing to *you*? Why?"

"Christmas and birthday cards," she said dryly. "Just look at it from a fund-raising point of view. Say you're an alum, and you see that your daughter's future headmaster takes the time to write her a birthday and Christmas card every year. Wouldn't *you* be more inclined to throw him a few extra bucks when it came time for the annual donation?"

Sure enough, Winnie was at the Marriott. He was engaged in some kind of very intense one-sided

conversation with that goth chick, Sarah Mullins—
Tony Viverito's girlfriend. Maybe he was just trying
to rip her off. Whatever was going on, Sarah didn't
seem very interested in what Winnie had to say. She
sat slumped in one of the rusted metal chairs,
wrapped in her black overcoat, puffing disinter-
estedly on a cigarette while Winnie stood over her,
frantically whispering and gesturing. Sunday strained
to listen, but she couldn't quite hear him.

"Hey, guys!" Fred called out.

Winnie froze. It occurred to Sunday that she
finally understood what the term "apple cheeked"
meant. His fat cheeks looked exactly like two red
apples. He shoved his hands in his pockets as Fred
and Sunday drew closer. "Hey," he called meekly.

"You!" Sarah spat at Fred. Her pale face soured.
She stood and ground her cigarette under one of
her Doc Martens.

"Hey," Fred said. "So, done any trust falls lately?"

"Don't talk to me," Sarah growled. She stormed
past them, back to the path that led to the Arts
Center. "Don't *ever* talk to me."

Fred hung his head. "I'll take that as a no," he
muttered.

Ouch, Sunday thought. Fred should have just kept
his mouth shut. Sarah hated him. But then, if
Sunday were Tony Viverito's girlfriend (*blecch*),

she'd hate Fred, too. There was no reason for Sarah *not* to hate Fred. Tony was gone; Fred was still here; and thanks to jerks like Winnie, people thought it was all Fred's fault. Sunday's jaw tightened. That was going to change, though. Yes, that was going to change very soon. Anger could be a good thing, she realized. It could be a lot more powerful than fear. And she was very afraid right now.

"That girl owes me twenty bucks for smokes," Winnie muttered, watching Sarah disappear. Then he smiled at Fred and Sunday. "So what's up? I didn't see you all weekend."

"We've been busy," Fred said.

"Yeah. Me, too. So what do you guys think about all the stuff that's been going on? Pretty crazy, huh? The whole campus is totally freaked. First Noah gets kicked out—"

"What happened with Noah, anyway?" Sunday interrupted. "I mean, I've heard rumors."

Winnie stared at her. Sunday's heart thumped under her Ralph Lauren suede jacket. This was a dangerous game of chicken they were playing. A very dangerous game. Because if Winnie suspected that Sunday knew the truth . . . well, it was best not to think about all that. She had to do this. She had to prove to herself that she could lie to Winnie without batting an eyelash. If she couldn't, this whole plan was doomed to fail from the get-go. She just had to think of this as an old-fashioned staring contest. And whoever blinked first—

Winnie laughed. "I heard that Noah slept with Miss Burke and made a videotape of it," he said offhandedly. "Who knew the kid had it in him? Although Spencer Todd told me that Miss Burke was a heroin addict. Which would also explain why she ran off with Mr. Burwell. You know, if that's what really happened. Oh, hey, Fred, who checked you in the past couple of nights?" Winnie couldn't seem to shut up. His tone was so strangely cheerful, too, as if they were just making the usual insipid small talk. "I mean, you don't have a dorm adviser anymore. That must be weird."

"Security is taking care of us," Fred said flatly. "Planet Biff and Sparkles are staying in Burwell's apartment." He stepped forward. "Look, man, you can relax. We know all about it. We know everything."

Winnie kept right on smiling. "What are you talking about?"

"You know what I'm talking about. I'm sure you figured out a long time ago that Sunday and I are on to you and Olsen."

"Uh . . . Fred, buddy? You haven't switched from dip to something stronger, have you?" Winnie chuckled. "Ha!" It sounded loud and wrong, like a broken car horn.

"So you're saying you had no idea that Sunday and I have been sneaking into Olsen's mansion and going through his stuff?" Fred asked.

Winnie's smile flickered—just for a second. His eyes seemed to glaze over. "Why would I have any idea about something like that?" he said.

Here it goes, Sunday said to herself.

She reached into her jacket pocket and pulled out the folded piece of stationery.

"All right, Winnie," she said. "Go ahead. Keep pretending that you don't know what we're talking about. That's fine with us. But it might interest you to know that Olsen plans to screw you. We found this in his rolltop desk last night, next to a pile of some very interesting papers and videotapes." She held out the letter.

"What is that?" Winnie asked. The cheery tone was gone.

"See for yourself," Fred said. "He was planning on mailing it tomorrow."

Winnie sneered. He marched forward and snatched the letter from Sunday. "I don't know what you guys think you're doing," he said as he unfolded it. "But if you want to mess with me, you're way out of your league. . . ." His voice trailed off as his eyes flashed across the paper.

Sunday held her breath. She cast a quick glance

at Fred. She could see the blood pulsating in the artery in his neck: *boom-boom-boom*. So. At least he seemed to be on the verge of a heart attack, too. She was starting to feel dizzy. God help them both. Winnie's expression hadn't changed. His face was a blubbery, surgically enhanced mask. He just kept reading. Very calmly. Very slowly. He wasn't buying the forgery. And if he didn't buy it—

"JESUS!" Winnie shouted.

Both Sunday and Fred flinched.

He glanced up at them. His face reddened. "Where the hell did you get this?"

"I told you," Sunday said. "Olsen's rolltop desk."

"That bastard," Winnie hissed. He stared into space, crumpling the letter in his hands. "He told me he was gonna kidnap Mackenzie."

"Excuse me?" Sunday said.

But Winnie didn't seem to hear her. In fact, he hardly seemed to notice that she and Fred were even there anymore. "He lied to me. That son of a bitch. He actually thinks he can double-cross me." Winnie threw the paper into the dirt. "There's no—"

"Wait, wait," Sunday interrupted. "What's this about Mackenzie?"

"Olsen was gonna kidnap her today. He's been going crazy, looking all over for her. He thinks he's screwed because . . ." He paused.

Any fleeting joy Sunday might have felt over having successfully duped Winslow Ellis instantly evaporated. Mackenzie was in danger. Serious danger. A man who fantasized about being the world's sexiest bachelor wanted to kidnap her.

"Because Sal Viverito wants his money?" Fred said. "Yeah. We know."

Suddenly, Winnie's demeanor changed. He didn't seem so angry anymore. Sunday couldn't tell *what* he was thinking. He looked as if he'd just taken a bite of spoiled meat.

Fred smiled. "Still think we're out of our league?"

"Wait—I-I don't get it," Winnie stammered.

"There's not much to get."

"You talked to Sal?" Winnie breathed.

"Of course we talked to Sal."

"What . . . what did he want?"

Fred laughed. "The question you should be asking is: What do *we* want?"

"Okay, what do *you*—"

"We want the freaking two hundred thousand, Winnie! What the hell do you think we want? You give *us* the money, or we send this letter to your parents and the cops. *With* the papers and videotape."

Winnie took a couple of steps back. His double chin was quivering. For the first time Sunday could remember, he actually appeared to be *scared*—as opposed to satisfied, or smug, or amused at somebody else's suffering. It would have pleased her, too—if she hadn't been so terrified herself. *Mackenzie.* Sunday had no idea where she was right now. Or Olsen, either, for that matter. He could have already gotten to her.

"You took the papers and videotape, too?" Winnie croaked.

Fred raised his eyebrows. "Come on. We're not amateurs. We made copies. One for us, one for the cops, one for your family. The way I see it, you're looking at ten years, minimum—"

"Okay. Okay. Just shut up. Let me think for a second." Winnie ran his chubby fingers through his blond hair, then turned to Sunday. "Sunday. Help me here. We've known each other since we were little kids. I mean—"

"Give it up, Winnie," Sunday groaned. "Just tell us where Mackenzie is."

"I honestly don't know. But she knows Olsen's looking for her."

Hmm. It wasn't the best answer, but it made Sunday feel a *little* better. After all, Mackenzie was terrified of Olsen, and she always had been—ever since she'd done his star chart. (And that was another thing Sunday would have to do when this whole thing was over: revisit her ideas about astrology.) So hopefully

Mackenzie was hiding somewhere. Hobson's room, maybe. In which case she'd probably already found Noah. But that was fine. The more, the merrier. She wouldn't risk getting cornered by Olsen alone.

"Well, Winnie," Fred said. "We'd love to stay and chat, but there's a little matter of two hundred thousand dollars." He tapped his watch. "Time is money, my man."

"You want it *now*?" Winnie shrieked.

"I'm not here to buy a tin of Old Hickory from you," Fred said.

"I . . . uh, well, getting the money isn't that easy. I don't even have access to that kind of cash. I mean . . ."

"Too bad," Fred said. He turned to Sunday. "Looks like we'll just have to tell the cops."

She shrugged. "Sounds good to me. Let's—"

"All right, all right," Winnie interrupted. "Jesus. If I'd known you guys were such scumbags, I would have made you my partners. I've got about twenty thousand stashed in the Caymans—"

"Twenty thousand?" Fred smirked. "You're lying."

"All right, maybe it's more like thirty, but—"

"Don't even try it."

"Okay, it's eighty. I swear."

"Do we look like chumps to you?" Fred asked.

"A hundred."

"Ha," Fred said.

"One twenty."

"You're insulting me, Winnie."

Sunday's eyes darted between the two of them. Winnie looked as if he were about to cry. His lips were jiggling. He sniffed and rubbed his eyes.

"Okay!" he shouted. "Okay! It's a hundred eighty, all right! I swear to God. But I've got to call the bank. I've got to close the account and arrange to transfer the funds."

"So bust out the cell phone," Fred said.

Winnie shook his head. "The cell phone? I don't know what you're talking—"

"Oh, shut up," Sunday snapped. She pointed at a phone-shaped bulge in the front pocket of his khakis. "Drop the dumb act. Make the goddamn call." Oddly, she was legitimately fed up. She was about to explode, in fact. She didn't know what was fueling her exasperation, either—impatience, contempt for Winnie, fear for Mackenzie . . . maybe some combination of all three. Or maybe she was just really getting into playing the role of a sleazy criminal. Anything was possible. She hadn't *slept*, for Christ's sake.

Fred smiled. "You heard the lady, Winnie," he said.

After wiping his nose on his shirt sleeve, Winnie kicked at the ground and yanked the slender black phone from his pocket. (He was actually pouting.

Sunday hadn't seen Winnie pout since he was five. She wished she could get this on tape.) He turned his back on the two of them and punched in a few numbers. The electronic *beep-bonk-bee-beep* sounded strangely out of place in the middle of the woods. Sunday looked up at the trees. She hadn't even noticed that autumn was really here. The foliage was gorgeous—those brilliant shades of red and orange and yellow that only last a couple of weeks, at most. It was funny what being preoccupied with a major conspiracy could make you forget. Like *life*, for instance.

"Yes, hello," Winnie said. His tone became clipped and formal. "M, please." There was a brief pause. "Account number zero-seven-seven-stroke-G-R-six-two-six-five-one-one-stroke-zero-three." He paused again. "Ophelia. Thank you."

Sunday glanced at Fred. Winnie's little monologue sounded like complete BS. For all they knew, he'd dialed a sex line, and some woman was panting in his ear right now.

Fred stepped forward and shoved his head next to the phone.

"What are you doing?" Winnie hissed. He swatted Fred's shoulder. "I——no, no, not you." He laughed uncomfortably. "Sorry. It's nothing. Bad connection." He strode to the other side of the clearing. "Yes. I'm here. Go on."

Sunday raised her eyebrows at Fred: *Well? Is it legit?*

Fred shrugged, then nodded, as if to say: *Sounds legit to me.*

A smile spread across Sunday's face. *Cool.* She couldn't help but feel a little tingle. She and Fred had actually reached the point where they could communicate without speaking. Fred smiled, too— although, of course, that was probably because they'd tricked Winnie into draining his own bank account. Still, the whole reading-minds thing was a fairly significant milestone in their relationship. Or maybe it wasn't. She had no idea, really, because she'd never been in a relationship before in her life. (And no, Boyce Sutton didn't count.) She wondered if Fred had ever carried on a silent conversation with what's-her-name.

Nah. Probably not.

"I'd like to close the account," Winnie said. "Oh, no? Why?" Winnie turned back toward Fred and Sunday and listened for a moment. "I see. Yes. Thank you very much." He closed the cell phone and shoved it back in his pocket. "The bank won't let me close the account over the phone," he said. "I need to be there in person."

"Crap," Fred muttered. He kicked at the leaves. "Crap, crap, CRAP!"

Sunday wasn't going to allow herself to give up or panic. Not when they'd gotten this far. It was weird, though. If Winnie had to close the account in person, he must have opened it in person—but she couldn't think of one time his family had gone to the Caribbean in the past few years. . . . *Wait a second.*

"Winnie, did you open the account yourself?" she asked.

"Yeah. *That* I could do over the phone."

"But they've never seen your face?"

He shook his head. "They don't even know my name. They've got serious secrecy laws down there— the accounts are all protected by a series of numbers, passwords, and security codes. They try to insulate themselves as much as possible from their clients. The less they know, the safer they are. That's why so many crooks use those banks to launder their money. But to close the account, I have to give all the information in person, so they can cut me a cashier's check. That's the problem."

"So what you're saying is: They have no idea what your name is, or what you look like," Fred said. He grinned at Sunday.

"Right." Winnie seemed confused. "So what?"

But Sunday already knew the answer. She grinned back at Fred. Yes, this mind-reading thing had definitely taken their relationship to a higher plane. Because she could tell exactly what Fred was thinking: Winnie didn't have to go to the Cayman Islands to get the money.

Somebody else could go for him. Somebody who didn't have to worry about missing any classes or checking into his dorm at night. Somebody who didn't even go to school.

Noah Percy's letter to his father

October 22

Dear Dad,

How are you? I am fine.

So. You're probably wondering why I haven't come home yet, seeing as I was expelled. You might also be wondering why some unusual charges have appeared on my Visa bill— among them a seersucker suit, the DVD of _Grease 2_, a subscription to _Ebony_ magazine, and round-trip first-class airfare from New York to the Cayman Islands.

If you haven't gotten the bill yet, I apologize in advance. In my defense, though, you told me I could use the card in emergencies. And I would say that I've had a lot of emergencies in the past week. I'm not exaggerating this time, either. I promise. It's not like the time I used the card to buy $800 worth of radial tires for that poor woman I met at the rest stop on I-95.

All right, now I feel guilty. I admit that the magazine charge wasn't technically an emergency, but I wanted to do something nice for Hobson because he's been letting me stay in his room. The same goes for the DVD. I stayed at the Winthrops' Lily Pond Lane residence for a few days, so I wanted to give Sunday a thank-you gift. Incidentally, you might want to mention to the Winthrops that they should think about a new cleaning service. Boy, what a sty! (Also, in case you were wondering, <u>Grease 2</u> is extremely underrated. Michelle Pfeiffer's in it. You love Michelle Pfeiffer. She was also in <u>Scarface</u>.)

Hey, can I ask you a question? I know you can't give me an immediate answer, but that's fine, because I want you to think about it. It's sort of deep.

When you're under a lot of stress, do certain patterns emerge? What I'm trying to say is, do you find that a lot of strange circumstances keep repeating themselves? Sort of like déjà vu?

Let me give you an example. Yesterday, I pretended to be somebody that I wasn't. I didn't give a false name or anything, but I said that I hated a guy named Noah Percy. (A Mafia hit man was waving a gun in my face at the time, so you can probably understand my motives.) And now I'm about to go on a trip where—yes, once again—I pretend to be somebody else.

Weird, huh?

Anyway, I miss these father-son chats. We should talk more.

Love,
Noah

P.S. I wanted to fly first class because my legs always fall asleep in coach. I hope that's okay. I'll send you a postcard when I'm down there.

P.P.S. If for some reason my body turns up at the bottom of a quarry or in some marsh in New Jersey, my final wish is this: Please make a really, really big deal out of my funeral. I want a "big bucks" casket, a "big bucks" organist playing a "big bucks" organ, and a "big bucks" tombstone in the shape of a giant toilet with a lit stick of dynamite sticking out of the bowl—you know, an eternal flame sort of thing, like at JFK's tomb. Thanks, Dad!!!

Part III
Karaoke Genius

7

Nobody makes a fool out of Allison Scott.

Allison repeated the words to herself as she strode down the vaulted marble hall toward Olsen's office. She'd opted for a toned-down, professional look today: a simple gray Miu Miu skirt and top with black tights. Her posture was stiff, her hair tied in a bun. Her Manolo Blahniks clattered on the floor.

Remember: You're in charge. You're the one who's holding the cards. You've got the upper hand—

Enough. This business of motivating herself with such hackneyed catchphrases was going to have to stop. It was beneath her. She *was* a senior at the Wessex Academy—still one of the finest preparatory schools in the country, in spite of the best efforts of its chief administrator to destroy everything it stood for.

No, make that *everything for which it stood*.

She wasn't going to use any more dangling prepositions, either. Or sentence fragments. Her command of the English language was in the 97th percentile, dammit—at least according to her standardized test scores. And for most of her life, she would have given Headmaster Olsen partial credit for that. *Ha!* She knew better now, though. Oh, yes. The only thing he could take credit for was distracting her with his dirty work. But she refused to let his corruption taint her education for another second. No, sir. She'd already wasted far too much time concerning herself with nonacademic matters. Because when all was said and done, she was here to *learn*.

Wasn't that why the Wessex Academy existed? For education? Wasn't the school supposed to be "dedicated to fostering the moral, intellectual, and physical development of its students"—as inscribed on page 2 of the hallowed Orientation Handbook? She'd already missed three classes today while rehearsing for this ridiculous confrontation with Olsen: Twentieth Century Lit (although that had probably been canceled, as Miss Burke was dead), Calculus, and Music of the Romantic Era. It was an outrage. Allison wasn't an *actress*. She was a student. She should be worrying about writing college essays—not worrying about tricking a sick old degenerate into thinking that one of his students, his coconspirator, had . . .

She clenched her fists at her sides.

Forget it. It was best not to think about Winnie. Or maybe she *should* think about him, just to remind herself how angry she was. To imagine for a second that she might have had some sort of rapport with him—that bloated, evil, iniquitous *hustler* . . . to imagine that she had thought they were bound by a profound understanding of their station in life, a station that none of their other friends ever seemed to comprehend . . . and to imagine that she had kissed him—*made out with him!*—yes, her anger over all that even surpassed her feelings toward Mackenzie and Hobson.

And she hadn't come close to forgiving *them*.

No, nobody ever made a fool out of Allison Scott. But somehow, Winnie had succeeded in doing just that. And he would pay. He would pay with what he loved most: money. She almost wished *she* could have handled him instead of Sunday and Fred. But no . . . no, it had to be done this way. She had to handle Olsen. Olsen trusted her. Besides, she didn't want to seem too obsessed with Winnie, because there was no way in hell she would ever let *anybody* find out that she had hooked up with him. *Ever.*

Except for Olsen. But that was part of the plan—her own, special, secret part.

Anyway, she wanted that goddamn cell phone.

She paused in front of Olsen's door.

It was closed—as always—and she could hear him on the other side, engaged in a hushed phone conversation. Typical. He was probably trying to squeeze another donation out of a poor, clueless parent. Or for all she knew, he was talking to a gangster. Or maybe he was blackmailing the Percys. It was truly amazing: Given everything she'd learned in the past twenty-four hours, she actually felt sorry for Noah. How could she not? He'd been set up—caught in the middle of this ugliness through no fault of his own, other than that his family had money and a good name. He'd been *shamed*. And no AB deserved that. Not even one as obnoxious and repellent as Noah Percy. But she was going to salvage that name—not only for his sake, but for the sake of *all* the sons and daughters of alumnae. That was why she was here. For the *real* Wessexonians.

She raised her fist to knock. Should she take one last peek in the mirror, just to make sure she looked secure and confident? No. It was best just to dive right in, while her adrenaline was pumping. She rapped on the door three times, very forcefully.

"Who is it?" Olsen called.

"Allison. May I come in?"

"Yes. Yes, of course." He muttered something else

into the phone, then slammed it down on the hook.

Allison pushed the door open and closed it behind her. "Hi," she said.

"Hello, Allison. I'm glad you stopped by."

Olsen had cleaned himself up quite a bit since yesterday. His clothes were pressed, the knot in his bow tie was crisp . . . yes, sitting there behind the oak desk, he almost appeared to be relaxed. Almost. A single strand of the attempted comb-over danced wildly above his head, caught in an updraft from the ceiling vent. She tried not to look at it, but it was mesmerizing—like a figure skater doing a pirouette. She perched on the edge of the leather couch so she could look him in the eye without craning her neck.

"Do you know where Mackenzie is?" Olsen asked, before she could even get settled. "It's very important that I talk to her."

"Mackenzie? She's probably in class." Allison glanced at the grandfather clock in the corner. It was just after two. "I think she has Art of the Renaissance now."

Olsen leaned across the desk. The dancing hair fell to his scalp. "She hasn't gone to a single class all day," he stated. "I've spoken with all of her teachers. I've been all over campus. She seems to have just vanished."

Allison swallowed. "Really. I . . . oh, my." She

tried to act calm, but this hadn't been part of the plan. Mackenzie didn't even *know* about the plan. "Maybe she's sick. Have you—"

"I've tried the infirmary as well."

"Oh," Allison said. "I had no idea."

"You can understand my concern, I'm sure," Olsen said. His eyes bored into her own. "I was very relieved to discover that Sunday had returned—although she will be disciplined, I can assure you—but in light of recent events . . ." He didn't finish.

Allison nodded.

"Miss Burke and Mr. Burwell are still missing," he continued in an ominous tone. "Strange goings-on are afoot, Allison."

"I know. I know." She shrugged. She didn't know what she was supposed to say. "You know, I'm sure Mackenzie's fine, though. Maybe she just decided to take the day off. She can be kind of flaky. I mean, you know that as well as anyone."

Olsen's face darkened. "'Pray, do not mock me,'" he quoted. "'I am a very foolish fond old man.'"

Try "disgusting old man," Allison thought. What was he even talking about? Was he trying to make her nervous? Yes, probably. He was spewing lines from *King Lear*, after all. But if she knew where Mackenzie was, she'd *tell* him. Her cheeks were beginning to ache from maintaining a blank expression.

"Mackenzie didn't say anything to you?" he pressed.

"No." Allison shook her head. "No, Headmaster Olsen." Her mouth was dry. Strangely, she felt like she was lying, even though she wasn't. "To tell you the truth, Mackenzie and I haven't really been talking much. We're sort of in a fight."

"Really?" Olsen leaned back in his chair. "Why?"

"Well, it's, um—it's complicated. I've been . . . um, seeing a bit of Winnie," she said. It made her sick just to utter the words. She had to do it, though.

"Winnie?" He seemed puzzled, but managed what almost looked like a smile. "I thought that you and Hobson were a pair."

Allison's lips tightened. "Yes. Well. So did I. That's part of the problem."

Olsen nodded slowly. "I see. Sorry, I don't mean to pry. This is none of my business."

"No, no. It's all right. That's also part of the reason I'm here."

"It is?" He frowned.

"Yes, Headmaster Olsen. You see, Winnie has told me some very strange things about you. And it's not in my nature to be a gossip—but as you said, in light of recent events, and because in the past, you've asked me to be forthcoming with certain information . . . well, I just thought it was best that you should know."

Olsen's jowls began to quiver. "Know what?"

"Well, he told me that you've been blackmailing students for hundreds of thousands of dollars and placing bets with the Mafia against the Wessex basketball team."

He stared at her. His flabby cheeks abruptly stopped shaking, as if he'd flipped an internal switch. "'And yet I know him a notorious liar,'" he said with a smile. "Remember that one? From *All's Well That Ends Well*?"

Allison shrugged. "Don't get me wrong. I don't think he's telling the truth, either. It definitely sounds too crazy to believe. But I just thought you should know what he's saying about you. He also said that he plans on going to the cops with proof that the Mafia paid you to kill Mr. Burwell and Miss Burke, and that their bodies are at the bottom of the old quarry out near Highway ninety-one."

"What?" Olsen cried.

"You know, the old quarry, out near—"

"I *know* where the old quarry is," he snapped.

Allison shrank back into the leather cushions. "Oh," she said sheepishly. "Sorry." She fought the temptation to smile. So Olsen wasn't as cool under pressure as she'd imagined him to be. He was definitely starting to crack. And it was all because of her. Now *this* was what it meant to be in control. She supposed she owed Sunday and Fred Wro—no, Fred *Wright*—an apology. Exercising power over the most powerful person at school was definitely . . . well, for want of a better word, a *rush*. Maybe she should have exercised that power more often. Maybe she shouldn't have been such a stickler for the rules. Not that the rules even *mattered*. Not when the person who enforced them was the biggest hypocrite on campus.

"It sounds to me like Winnie needs help," Olsen said. He fiddled with his bow tie. He was starting to sweat. Little drops of perspiration appeared on his upper lip. "His behavior has been quite erratic recently. I've noticed it myself. Perhaps the boy could benefit from some counseling. Fall term senior year is an extremely stressful time."

Allison raised her eyebrows. "Winnie? In counseling? You mean, like, seeing a shrink?"

Olsen scowled at her. "Yes, Allison. It's nothing to be ashamed of."

"I didn't say it was."

"You know how stressful this time is. This is when your performance matters most. Colleges are watching you. They're looking to pick the cream of the crop."

"I know," Allison said.

Olsen leaned across the desk again. "Allison, this is an extremely sensitive matter. I'm sure I don't have to tell you that if a student of Winnie's status is indeed suffering some kind of episode, we need to respect his family's privacy. He's a member of the student council, after all. I'm extremely grateful that you came forward, but it's best that we keep this among ourselves. You understand, don't you?"

Allison nodded. "Oh, yes, of course," she said. *Sucker!* she added silently.

"Did he say anything else?" Olsen asked, searching her eyes. "Anything at all?"

"Hmm. Let me think. . . ." Allison stroked her chin. "Oh, yeah. He did say one thing. He said that the only way you could possibly stop him was if you readmitted the kids you framed. You know, Noah and Tony Viverito. He said that he was being threatened by . . . by . . ." She snapped her fingers. It was getting harder and harder not to laugh. "I can't—"

"Sal Viverito?" Olsen asked.

Allison tilted her head. "Yeah." She acted confused. "I don't get it. Why Sal Viverito? He's a respected alum, isn't he? Why would he threaten anybody?"

"He *wouldn't* threaten anyone, Allison," Olsen whispered. His jowls were shaking again. "Winnie's whole story is complete and utter balderdash. He's been fixated on Sal ever since Sal's younger brother was expelled. It's part of Winnie's . . . *breakdown*. The poor boy is deluded. He needs professional care."

"Really." Allison shook her head gravely. "I was hoping it wasn't that bad."

"It's bad all right," Olsen muttered. He spun around in his chair so that he was facing the window. "It's very, very bad."

Allison smiled. *And it's only going to get worse—* She stopped in midthought. *No more hackneyed catchphrases,* she reminded herself. That was Olsen's department. She stood up from the couch. "Well, I should be getting to class. What should I do about Winnie?"

Olsen swiveled back to her, his face creased with worry. "What do you mean, *do* about him?"

"I should probably keep an eye on him, you know?"

"Yes. Yes, of course." He nodded, distracted. "You're his friend, after all. He needs your support. But if you wouldn't mind . . . well, not to sound indelicate or insensitive—"

"Reporting back to you?"

He smiled gratefully. "You understand everything, Allison."

"Yeah." She chewed her thumbnail, pretending to think for a moment. "You know, Winnie says that he's on a special committee of yours that permits him to use a cell phone."

Olsen's smile disappeared. Once again, the lone hair began to dance over his head.

"Anyway, I think it might be a good idea if *I* had a

140

cell phone, Headmaster Olsen," she continued, looking at him directly. "You know, just in case if Winnie
has some sort of emotional collapse, and I need to
notify you immediately. I'd only use it in emergencies, of course."

He blinked several times. "Of course," he
echoed flatly.

"So is that all right? Do I have your permission
to buy a cell phone?"

"Well. I suppose, since the circumstances are
rather extraordinary—"

"Great!" she exclaimed. "I'll pick it up at Value
City and charge it to the school account. And if I
see Mackenzie, I'll send her your way." She turned
and reached for the doorknob.

"Allison?"

"Yes?"

"The entirety of this conversation must be kept
in the strictest of confidence."

She cast a sly grin over her shoulder. "' 'Tis a secret
must be locked within the teeth and the lips,'" she
quoted. "Remember that one? From *Measure for Measure*?"

He didn't answer. But then, he didn't have to. It
was a rhetorical question—much like: *You know who's
running the show now, don't you?*

Yes, yes, yes.

Allison closed the door. Mission accomplished.

Letter from Headmaster Olsen
to Carmine Viverito

The Honorable Headmaster Phillip Olsen
The Wessex Academy
41 South Chapel Street
New Farmington, Connecticut 06744

Mr. Carmine Viverito
1 Stone Hill Terrace
Quogue, NY 11244

October 23

Dear Carmine,

I am writing to offer my most sincere apologies for having dismissed your son, Anthony. The mistake was ours, and I take sole responsibility for it. Yesterday, one of our students confessed to having planted the chewing tobacco in Anthony's bag. Owing to certain rules of confidentiality, I cannot divulge the offending student's name—but I can assure you that he is packing his bags for home as I write this letter.

As of this moment, all charges have been officially expunged from Anthony's record.

In short, we would be delighted to have him readmitted as soon as possible. While I understand that you must be angry and upset with us, with excellent reason, please remember that a diploma from the Wessex Academy represents the highest in academic, moral, and physical achievement at the secondary school level. I can't think of anyone more deserving of an opportunity to graduate and receive this diploma than your son.

I look forward to hearing from you soon.

Sincerely,
The Honorable Phillip Olsen

8

The momentous vision came to Noah just after he had cleared customs. He was standing in the taxi line outside the airport on Grand Cayman—with the warm Caribbean breeze whipping through his curls and the sun already poisoning his skin with deadly carcinogens (*ahh, that's the stuff*) . . . when, suddenly, without warning, it hit:

He would have to play himself in the film version of his life.

Of course he would. Who else could do it? Who else could wear this white seersucker suit with such panache? Who else combined such a devastating blend of style and sex appeal in a single five-foot-ten, hundred-and-twenty-pound frame? In a word: nobody. And that face. No one had a face like

Noah's. His was a face with character. (Character in this instance meaning a big red zit to the left of his nose.) But, hey, blemish-free Hollywood cheekbones were a dime a dozen. The *Noah Percy Saga*—a biopic series that would surpass even the *Godfather* films in terms of accolades—was deserving of something more. This series would change cinema as a whole, with its intimate indie feel on an action-flick budget. . . .

Or . . .

Or maybe he'd had too many free mimosas.

Noah swayed in his loafers. It was a good thing he hadn't brought any luggage besides a briefcase. He'd packed light—just a pair of boxer shorts, his unfinished Wesleyan application (in case he got bored), and Winnie's copy of *The Criminal's Guide to Offshore Bank Accounts*. He didn't want to be weighed down.

He hadn't wanted to drink on the flight, either. But after riding so many trains, he felt he owed it to himself to sample all the pleasures that planes had to offer . . . and besides, he hadn't even *asked* for the first mimosa. The stewardess just handed it to him with that lovely, tropical smile. Before the plane even took off! Then the singing started. There were only five other passengers on the flight—all in their thirties—and they all wanted to *sing*. Bob Marley songs, mostly. Fortunately, Noah was additionally blessed with a lovely singing voice and a firm command of the entire Bob Marley repertoire, so he'd felt obligated to take their impromptu a capella jam to a higher level.

And he had. Boy, had he ever. For that flight, he'd *been* Bob Marley.

"Wo-yo-yo! Wo-yo-yo-yo. . . ."

Anyway, as far as *NPS: Part II* was concerned, the rest of the cast was already in place. Allison, obviously, would be played by Nicole Kidman. Hobson would be played by Eminem. Or maybe Will Smith. Sunday . . . *hmm*. That was a tough call. He'd have to give that some thought. For Fred, he was thinking either Tom Hanks or—

"Where to, mon?"

Noah jumped.

A Rastafarian was standing right in front of him. *Whoa.* Speaking of Bob Marley . . . this guy looked almost exactly like him—the long dreadlocks, the bloodshot eyes, the works. He even spoke with the same thick Jamaican accent.

"I'm sorry," Noah said. "What was that?"

The guy waved at a tiny red taxicab. The color matched his Hawaiian shirt. "Where to? Downtown?"

"Uh . . . yeah."

"Right on. Hop in, mon."

Noah's head swam. He was in no position to

argue. He was buzzed; he was in a foreign country; he was pretending to be Winslow Ellis. Sort of. And the day had started so *normally*, too. Up at four in the morning, out of Hobson's sleeping bag, a steaming bowl of ramen noodles to get him on his way—

"You comin'?"

Noah tossed his briefcase into the back seat and dove in behind it.

The driver peeled out of the airport and onto a seaside highway. Noah bounced around in the back seat. He felt like a pinball. The cab didn't seem to have any shocks. It didn't have any air-conditioning, either. He rolled down the window. The air felt a lot muggier and more humid blasting into his face than it had back on the curb.

"Hey, I'm sorry," Noah called to the driver. "I don't mean to be a pain, but aren't you driving on the wrong side of the road?"

The driver burst out laughing. "You funny, mon!" he shouted back.

Noah smiled, gripping the door in terror. He wasn't trying to make a joke. He stared out the window at the passing cars and the colorful, tin-roofed shanties. The ocean beyond was a beautiful, turquoise blue. Luckily, *everybody* seemed to be driving on the wrong side of the road. Then he remembered: The Cayman Islands were a British Colony. Everything was done backward. He breathed a sigh of relief. *Whew.* Now all he had to worry about was successfully defrauding a bank out of nearly two hundred thousand dollars.

"So where you goin'?" the driver yelled.

"The Federated Bank of Georgetown," Noah yelled back.

The driver's stoned gaze met Noah's in the rearview mirror. He seemed puzzled. "You here on business, mon?"

"You could say that."

"You look too young to be doin' any kinda business."

Noah shrugged. "I *feel* too young," he said.

The driver laughed again. He leaned forward and flicked on the radio. The opening chords of Bob Marley's "Buffalo Soldier" blasted from the speakers.

Noah bolted upright. "I don't believe it!" he cried. He slapped the back of the driver's seat. "I was singing this song on the flight down! This exact song . . ." He slumped back again. "Sorry. Guess you had to be there."

"Good things come in twos," the driver said.

"What was that?"

The driver looked to the rearview mirror and nodded solemnly, as if imparting some bit of sacred, mystical wisdom. "They say that good things come in threes, but it's not true, mon. Good things come in *twos*. Remember that."

Noah nodded back. "Thanks," he said. He *would* remember that. Until now, he'd always assumed that only bad things came in twos. But that was just because everything in his life was bad. Maybe this guy was onto something, though. After all, what could be bad about Bob Marley? Absolutely nothing. *Right on, mon,* Noah told himself. He grinned drunkenly. It was about freaking time his luck started changing. Today might just be the day.

The Federated Bank of Georgetown was on one side of a wide square with about a zillion other banks. It was a little weird. As far as Noah could tell, there didn't seem to be any other buildings in this town *besides* banks. They all looked alike, too—big, low, and glassy—but they all seemed to come from different countries. Not that he particularly cared about the multinational scenery. He just wanted to get the money and get the hell out before his buzz wore off. He needed all the liquid courage he could muster.

A pretty blond woman in a dark business suit approached him as soon as he stepped into the lobby. She looked a little like Christina Aguilera, only older and stuffier and with glasses. Everyone in this country seemed to resemble a beautiful celebrity.

"Can I help you, young man?" she asked cheerfully, with a trace of an English accent.

Young man. Noah hated when people called him that. This woman was probably Miss Burke's age. He'd *slept* with a woman that old. True, the woman had been damaged and evil (rest in peace), but still.

"Yes." He cleared his throat. He wanted to speak in as deep a voice as possible. "Thank you. I'm here to close my account."

She eyed him dubiously. "You have an account *here*?"

"Yes. Well. Normally, I conduct my banking in the States, but I had a little trouble with the SEC after some of the stocks I promoted went south," he said. "You might have read about me in the paper. 'Teen Stock Swindler'? The charges were all false, of course. But I wanted to protect my money. You understand."

The woman smiled. "I think I did read about that." She gave him another quick look up and down. "That was *you*?"

"Yes." Noah shrugged modestly. He had no idea where that little speech had come from. He thought for sure she was going to call security and have him escorted from the building.

"You know, I believe we spoke briefly on the phone yesterday," the woman said. She extended a bony hand. Noah shook it. "I'm Marcia Burke. I'd be happy to help you with your account. This way, please."

Noah stared at her. "Did you say . . . Burke?"

"Yes. Why?"

"No reason." He flashed a queasy smile. *Only good things come in twos,* he told himself. *Not bad things. Only good things. . . .*

He followed her into a little cubicle and sat on the other side of her desk, facing the back of a computer monitor. The name was just a coincidence. That was all. A very unfortunate coincidence. Anyway, she wasn't Miss Burke. She was Marcia.

"Do you mind if I call you Marcia?" he asked.

"Of course not." She peered at the screen and began to type. "And you are . . . ?"

"Winslow Ellis," Noah said.

"And why are you closing your account, if I may ask, Mr. Ellis?"

Noah blinked. That was a very good question. And he didn't have the slightest idea how to answer it. He'd been too preoccupied with memorizing the passwords and stupid codes . . . and how the hell had Fred and Sunday talked him into flying down here in the first place? He had no business sitting in a Caribbean bank. He had no business talking to this woman. He should be at home right now. Or at least back in Hobson's room, chilling in that bathrobe.

An extremely unpleasant feeling swept over him. It was the same sort of thing he'd felt in Miss Burke's apartment the night she'd seduced him: the sudden, sickening realization that he was nothing more than a *child*—and a scared, angry, victimized child at that.

"You don't have to answer, of course," Marcia said in a soothing tone. "I was just concerned you were dissatisfied with our service."

"Oh, no. No. Not at all. Of course not. I . . . ah—well, I just wanted to be more *liquid*." He smiled, feeling like an idiot.

"Of course. I understand perfectly."

I'm glad one of us does. Noah didn't know how much longer he could maintain this level of BS. Thank God the air-conditioning in this place was cranked. Otherwise, he would have sweated clear through his suit by now.

"Can I have your account number, please?" she asked.

Noah nodded. "Zero-seven-seven-stroke-G-R-six-two-six-five-one-one-stroke-zero-three," he said.

"I'm sorry, can you repeat the last five digits, please?"

"Five-one-one-stroke-zero-three."

He was surprised by how smoothly he'd rattled that off. It was a good thing he'd repeated all this stuff to his reflection for about four straight hours last night.

"Very good," Marcia said. "And the password?"

"Ophelia."

She smiled as she typed. "That's pretty."

"I think so," Noah said.

"Date of birth?"

Noah opened his mouth—and just barely caught himself. He'd been about to give her *his* date of birth, not Winnie's. "Eight, seventeen, eighty-three," he said.

She punched in the numbers. "All right, Mr. Ellis. Your mother's maiden name?"

"Eaton," he said.

"And finally, your personal security code."

"Nineteen-thirty-four, eighteen-eighty-nine," Noah replied. He remembered those numbers easiest of all, because they were the years that Charles Manson and Hitler were born, respectively. Leave it to Winnie to choose *that* as his personal security code.

"Fine." She tapped one last key, then leaned back in her chair. The screen flickered. Her eyes widened. "My goodness."

Noah felt a twinge of panic. "Yes? Is there a problem?"

She smiled and turned to him. "Excuse me, no. It's just that . . . nothing. I'm sorry we'll be losing your business. That's all."

"Oh." He laughed. So. There *was* no problem. It was done. Done! In less than a minute. How easy had *that* been? He was hardly even conscious of what had happened. He almost wanted to repeat the whole procedure, just really *process* it. Well, no, not really. But if he hadn't been about to pass out, he would have jumped up and thrown his hands over his head in a wild and demented dance of victory. (Or not.) He couldn't believe this. He was a born swindler. He would *definitely* have to play himself in the movie.

"You're certain you want to close the account all at once?" Marcia asked.

"I'm sure. They don't call me 'Big Bucks Winnie' for nothing."

"Will a cashier's check be all right?" she asked.

"I'd rather have cash," he said.

She blanched. "Pardon?"

"Cash. Bills. Paper. That's what it means to be liquid, doesn't it?"

"Well, yes, I suppose so—but aren't you concerned about security?" She shot a nervous glance toward the bank lobby, then leaned across the desk. "You're talking about one hundred eighty-seven thousand U.S. dollars. I'm not even sure we have that amount on the premises."

He shrugged, feigning disappointment. The truth was, he didn't really care. He'd just thought it would be cool to carry around a briefcase full of cash for a day. This *was* a high-stakes sting operation, after all, and he needed to behave with a certain amount of stupidity in order to feel ironically detached from the rest of the plan—otherwise, he would think too seriously about what he still had to pull off (meaning giving the money to Sal), and he would wet his pants. A cashier's check just didn't cut it. It was too formal. Too *real*. And frankly, it just wasn't glamorous enough. In the film version of this event, he would definitely get cash.

"I really don't think it's such a good idea, Mr. Ellis," she said.

"Why? Are you thinking about robbing me?"

"No, no." She blushed. "It's just—"

"Fine. You can cut me a cashier's check."

"I'm sorry to disappoint you," she said.

"Well, I'll tell you what. I'll let you make it up to me. I'm staying at The Palms on Seven Mile Beach. Why don't you join me there for dinner tonight? I'm only here until tomorrow, and I don't know anyone in town."

She stared at him. Her face turned even redder.

Noah honestly didn't know what had come over him. Maybe it was the mimosas talking. Maybe it was because her name was Burke. Maybe it was that he would actually be walking out of here with Winnie's ill-gotten fortune. But he really hadn't meant to embarrass her like that. He didn't even *want* to have dinner with her tonight. He just wanted to order room service and watch *American Pie 2* on cable. Not that he was in any danger of her accepting. After all, he was a "young man." With a zit on his cheek, no less. Oh, well. It was probably just the same old asinine reflex that compelled him to blow up toilets. When things are going well, why not screw them up? He was an expert—

"What time shall I meet you?" she asked.

"How's eight o'clock?"

"Perfect."

Only a certain rare breed of genius truly understood the art of karaoke—and Noah meant "art" in the most profound sense of the word. There were always the hacks, the one-timers, the drunks, the bloated yuppies at their bachelor parties . . . but every now and then, a true *singer* would step up to the plastic microphone, and the entire room would fall silent, rapt with attention—with *awe*, really—having never heard a performance of the Led Zeppelin's seminal "Stairway to Heaven" so bawdy or impassioned.

Marcia Burke is my ideal woman.

Noah wasn't kidding himself. He was a hair's breadth away from weeping. And this time it wasn't because of any free drinks. He was stone cold sober.

Truth be told, up until they'd stumbled accidentally into the karaoke room while searching for the toilets, he'd written off the entire night as a wash. All Marcia had talked about over dinner (his treat) was garbage along the lines of: "I don't see myself as a bank officer ten years down the road." Fine. Great. For Christ's sake, he didn't see himself as a puppeteer, but there was no reason to *talk* about it. He'd snored politely through the entire conversation, hoping to ditch her after the check came. But then they'd found this place, this tiny little wonderland, and she'd slipped the DJ her little scrap of paper and walked up under those lights. . . . Well, he'd just had no idea. You could never tell about a person. Ever.

"That was incredible," he said to her as soon as she sat back down. He had to practically scream to make himself heard over the applause and hooting of the twenty or so fans she'd just made. He leaned over their tiny candlelit table. "Are you a professional singer or something?"

"Oh, no, no, no," she muttered. She laughed and stared down at her lap. "It's just something I do for fun. Really."

"Well, if you're looking to switch careers, I think you found your calling."

"Oh, go on," she said. "I think you're just a big Zeppelin fan."

He shook his head. "No, no, not at all. Well, you know—I used to be. But I sort of think of bands the way I think of girlfriends, you know? You're introduced—and there's this period of intense passion, when you can't stop thinking about them. Then you settle into a comfy routine. Then things either stay comfy or they go sour. And if they go sour . . . well, eventually you either feel nostalgic for them, or you pretend they never existed."

She laughed. "And how is it with Zeppelin?"

"Nostalgic. Definitely nostalgic. But with a band like Bon Jovi, you know—it's sort of embarrassing to admit that I was ever involved with . . ."

Fortunately, his voice was lost in the cacophony. Everybody started clapping in unison. "More, more, more," they chanted. "More, more, more . . ."

"I think your audience is demanding an encore," Noah yelled.

She smiled up at him. "Would you like to join me?"

Noah's face reddened. "What—um, you mean, like, *sing*?"

"Well, we don't have to sing. We could do a rap number. 'Gin 'n' Juice.' I could be Dr. Dre, and you could be Snoop Dogg."

Noah stared at her. Marcia Burke wasn't just *his* ideal woman. She was womanhood perfected. "Wait a sec," he said. "You're not just saying you want me to be Snoop because I'm so much younger than you, are you?"

She laughed. "Younger? What's four years? You're eighteen; I'm twenty-two. Dre has a good six years on Snoop, at least."

"Good point," Noah said. Actually, he was seventeen—but there was no reason to nitpick.

"More, more, more . . ."

"Come on!" the DJ shouted. "Get up here!"

"What do you say, Winnie?" Marcia asked.

Winnie! Jesus. Noah had almost forgotten that he was Winslow Ellis. Good thing she'd reminded him. He smiled. It was odd how life worked out sometimes. Before tonight, if somebody had told him that he would be forced to become Winnie for a day, he probably would have reacted a lot like that bulb-headed figure in Edvard Munch's *The Scream*. But now he wasn't so sure. Winnie knew how to have a good time. He was a high roller. He was no child, either. He could charge hundreds on his father's Visa card, hold his own with a lady like Marcia Burke—*and* rock the microphone, all in one night. And who knew where a night like that could lead?

"Let's go, then." She extended a hand over the table. "We'll do a duet. Another Zeppelin song, if you like. Good things come in twos, you know."

Noah clasped her delicate fingers. "Yeah," he said. "I heard that once."

Another segment of Noah Percy's Wesleyan application

Part 4: In a single paragraph, please describe what you would consider to be the defining moment of your life thus far.

I know what you're thinking. Having read my previous essay, you would think that the defining moment of my life thus far was when I lost my virginity to that foul seductress of a teacher (rest in peace). Not so, my Wesleyan friends, not so. The defining moment of my life is right now! Because it is only now, in this hotel room, with the Caymanian (is that a word?) sunshine streaming through the curtains and this beautiful woman sleeping beside me (shhh! I have to write quietly), that I see the truth. The taxi driver who picked me up at the airport yesterday was no ordinary man, but indeed a mystic, a prophet—his uncanny resemblance to Bob Marley being no mere coincidence. More to the point, the seemingly trite aphorism he uttered was in fact sacred wisdom, the words by which I will judge all the events of my life henceforth: "Good things come in twos." Like sex with twenty-two-year-old bombshells named Burke, for example.

Does that make any sense?

Oops! More than one paragraph. Forget that question.

Part IV
Eye of Newt

9

Burglarizing a home was not a crime Winslow Ellis had ever imagined himself committing. It was so pedestrian. Although, this wasn't *really* a burglary, as he had no intention of stealing anything. He only wanted to move a few items to a more suspicious-looking location inside Olsen's house.

Still, professionals insulated themselves from their nefarious deeds, just like the bankers who laundered their money. At the same time, however, he recognized the need to do whatever was necessary in order to ensure survival. He never let survival interfere with pride. For most of his eighteen years—or at least since he'd been taking advantage of the imbeciles who surrounded him—he'd lived his life by two simple rules, both of which were dedicated to self-preservation.

1) "Never underestimate the other guy's greed."
2) "Never get high on your own supply."

Yes, he'd stolen the rules directly from *Scarface*. But it was his right to do so.

Furthermore, in spite of what Hobson may have claimed, Winnie was the one who had first seen the movie and introduced it to everyone. Somehow, the long-standing rumor was that this had been Hobson's coup. It was part of the nonofficial Wessex lore.

As if Hobson could appreciate the film on all its levels. As if he could understand the brilliant combination of Brian De Palma's directing, Oliver Stone's writing, and Al Pacino's acting. As if *Hobson Crowe*—a boy who still thought that playing the role of a "white homey" was something fresh, new, and controversial—could possibly understand the true genius of the movie, how it had captured that special moment in the early '80s when morality was for suckers and money was king.

Ridiculous.

Perhaps the rumor was founded in truth. Winnie didn't know, and he didn't particularly care. He *did* know, however, that truth was what you made it. Believe in something for long enough; convince people that it was real—and the truth could be as malleable as a piece of clay. If he made the right moves, by the end of the year, he would have everyone believing what *he* believed: *Scarface* had been *his* discovery. In any event, Hobson had no right claiming the film as his own. He didn't live by its rules.

Rule number two was figurative, really, as Winnie had never touched drugs and never would. To use drugs was to open oneself to attack. Even smoking or dipping compromised one's power. No, his "supply" was the money he'd earned: the fortune that until this afternoon had been safely stowed in an offshore bank account—and would be stowed there again shortly, as soon as he'd figured out how to dispose of Sunday, Fred, and Noah.

Winnie wiped the sweat from the bridge of his nose.

It was nearly four A.M., but he'd rarely felt so wide-awake. He crept silently through Olsen's darkened kitchen, his gloved hands in front of him. *Vulnerability is for the weak*, he said to himself. He was paraphrasing Genghis Khan. He did this at times when he needed a little extra kick of adrenaline, a little reminder of who he really was: a predator. For all time, throughout all human history, the world had been divided into the predators and the prey. Society was built upon this division. Without it, civilization would crumble. It *was* crumbling. One only needed to take a look around the campus to see that the predators had grown soft, so the prey were free to run wild—to skip class, to disappear, to bring the Wessex Academy to the brink of chaos. . . .

The prey must be destroyed. And Olsen with them.

It was a good thing nobody could see him right now—in part, because he was wearing a Halloween ninja outfit he'd stolen from the theater department, but mostly because he couldn't hide his rage any longer, even *with* the ninja hood and face mask. The rage was in his eyes. He was enraged at everyone: at Fred and Sunday for attempting to blackmail him, at Noah for going to the Cayman Islands and stealing his "supply" (temporarily, of course). . . . Yet most of all, he was enraged at himself. Intoxicated by three straight years of triumph and profit—*three straight years*—he'd slipped. He'd allowed himself to forget Rule Number One. He *had* underestimated the other guy's greed.

In his own defense, though, he'd never imagined Olsen could be so treacherous. Winnie had long since planned for an act of betrayal on Olsen's part—only an idiot wouldn't, given the peculiar nature of their joint venture—but he'd never really believed Olsen would make the first move in a crisis. Especially one as shrewd and devious as that letter. Winnie had forgotten that he himself would have sunk to the exact same level. Correction: He'd forgotten he *should* have sunk to the exact same level. Pride and hubris had dulled his edge.

But the fight was just beginning. He'd learned from his mistakes. He would be damned if he let that retirement-aged sideshow freak get the best of him. Sure, he had lots to hide. But so did Olsen. And only *he* knew Olsen's secrets. Only *he* knew what Olsen did and hid in that basement. Sunday and Fred may have caught a glimpse of it, but Winnie alone knew the true depths of Olsen's warped brain.

He sneered as he tiptoed past the rolltop desk in the living room. The old kook would rue the day he'd threatened the Ellis family. Because Winslow Ellis had a few secrets of his own. Oh, yes, he did. And if Olsen wanted to play hardball, that was fine by him. He was ready.

The cellar stairs were pitch black, but Winnie had been up and down them so many times that it didn't matter. When he reached the bottom step, he dug into the pocket of his baggy black pants and pulled out a tiny flashlight. He clicked it on, aiming the beam across the "basketball court" to the trophy case—

He jerked.

The trophies.

Something was wrong. Very wrong.

He dashed forward.

The top shelf . . . it was empty.

Okay. Relax. Deep breaths. One, two, three. In and out. Repeat. Predators didn't panic. They dealt. Maybe Olsen had just moved the trophies to another shelf . . . yes? Please? No. He hadn't. Winnie swung the flashlight around the room. They weren't in a corner, or in a new case, or under the nets. . . . Could Olsen have sent them out to get cleaned or polished? Or taken them upstairs?

Winnie gave the case another search. Just to double-check. Just to make sure this wasn't some horrible mistake.

They were gone. So was that ugly little treasure chest, for some reason. Not that he cared about that. *Dammit!* There was no way Olsen could have foiled him again. There was no way Olsen could have suspected what those trophies *really* were. How could he? They were cheap gifts! Symbols of victory! The spoils of war! Winnie had given the first one to Olsen as a "memento." It had been right after that first Operation Time Capsule, when they'd successfully gypped Grady Thomas's parents out of 75 Gs of "hush money" after convincing them that he was the biggest Ecstasy dealer east of the Rockies—

But now was not the time to reminisce. Winnie had to compartmentalize. Shove the distractions to one side, focus on the task at hand. The trophies had to be around here somewhere. They were never supposed to leave this basement. That was why he'd chosen *trophies* in the first place: to fill up Olsen's freaking cabinet. Olsen loved goddamn awards. Even if they were fake. They were safe down here. They were protected by Olsen's unflappable delusions of grandeur.

Or so Winnie had assumed.

He turned off the light and hurried back up the stairs. The old man was turning out to be a slippery son of a bitch. But that was fine. Technically, Winnie didn't need the trophies. They would have helped, though. A lot. His plan had been to stow them somewhere else in the house, somewhere a lot more safe and suspicious-looking. That way, Olsen wouldn't know where they were. Although . . . Sunday and Fred had mentioned finding a mother lode in the rolltop desk. Maybe Olsen had hidden the trophies there as well. If not, maybe Winnie could bluff his way into convincing—

"Hello, Winslow."

He was blinded by a sudden, brilliant white glare.

"What the—" His voice was muffled by the face mask. He staggered back in the narrow corridor, blinking and squinting. Purple dots swam before his eyes. Olsen was pointing some kind of industrial-strength flashlight directly in his face. "Jeez! Turn that thing off, all right?"

"What, may I ask, are you doing in my home?" Olsen demanded.

"Nothing."

Olsen laughed grimly. "Nothing, eh? Then why are you wearing that absurd costume?"

"I'm playing dress-up," Winnie muttered. He lumbered blindly into the light, shoving his way past Olsen into the front hall. "You can understand that. It's the same reason you wear that basketball uniform."

"I'm in no mood for this right now, Winslow. It's four in the morning." Olsen turned off the flashlight and flicked on the overhead lamp. "I can only assume you're dressed this way because you didn't want to be spotted violating curfew and coming to my house. So why don't you just tell me what you're looking for."

Winnie turned and scowled at him. "I'm not looking for anything, dammit." He glanced through the archway at the rolltop desk. "I just—"

"You just what?"

"Never mind." He headed for the living room. "Why don't you go back to bed?"

Click.

Well, well.

This was an intriguing development. Winnie was tempted to laugh. Olsen had drawn a gun on him. A small, snub-nosed pistol—a .22, by the looks of it. In his pajamas and bathrobe. How very cute, to quote Olsen himself. How very New-England-Republican-homeowner-exercising-his-right-to-bear-arms.

"Tell me what you're looking for," Olsen commanded.

"What if I don't? Are you going to shoot me?"

"Don't tempt me," Olsen said. "It would make my life a lot easier."

"Is that why you wrote that letter to my parents?" Winnie asked.

The bags under Olsen's eyes seemed to darken. "Letter? I have no idea what you're talking about."

Winnie sighed. "Come on, Phil. You can do better than that."

"That's Headmaster Olsen to you."

"Ooh, so *that's* how we're playing it now." Winnie smiled. "What about that conversation we had freshman year? Gosh. I still remember it so well. It started as just an idea—you know, a student and his principal talking, shooting the breeze, and then . . . well, then it got a little dark—"

"Shut up. Tell me what you're after, or so help me God, I'll kill you."

Winnie's smile brightened. Used in the right way, a smile could be far more threatening than any weapon. Olsen truly *was* pathetic. As if Winnie would be scared by that gun! No, Olsen was far more afraid right now. His fear was written all over those trembling jowls.

"I'm really disappointed, *Headmaster Olsen*," Winnie

said, emphasizing the last two words. He stepped toward him. "This is so dramatic. There has to be some appropriate quote you can pluck from the Shakespeare canon to—"

"Stop it," Olsen breathed. He raised the pistol. "Don't come any closer."

"Take it easy, all right?" Winnie was less than a yard away from him.

Olsen thrust the barrel at Winnie's forehead, but his hand was shaking so much that there was about a one percent chance a bullet would even come close. Winnie liked those odds. He wasn't much of a gambler, after all. That was Olsen's specialty. He kept his eyes fixed on Olsen's, his face a picture of contentment. Then, without so much as a blink, he struck out with his left hand and snatched the gun from Olsen's grasp.

"Hey!" Olsen shrieked.

He lunged at Winnie. The two of them went toppling to the floor.

Ow! Winnie struck his elbow, right in the funny bone. An excruciating tingle shot up his arm. He winced. *Jesus*, that hurt. The gun slipped a little. It was heavier than he'd imagined. Olsen was right on top of him. Winnie kicked, squirming to get out from under the guy—and thankfully managed to plant his right knee right in Olsen's crotch.

"Oof!" Olsen groaned. His body went limp.

Winnie shoved himself free and jumped to his feet, breathing heavily. He teetered for a moment, pointing the gun down at Olsen's tired and agonized old face.

Olsen crumpled into a fetal position.

"That was stupid, Phil," Winnie panted. He wanted to prolong this sweet moment of torture, but he knew he shouldn't. "Tell me where the trophies are."

Olsen moaned. "What trophies?"

"The O.T.C. trophies! Where did you move them?"

"I have no idea what you're talking about."

Winnie grabbed the gun with both hands to steady it. "Stop lying to me."

"Why would I touch those trophies?" Olsen asked. He crawled over to the archway to pull himself to his feet. "They've never left my trophy case."

"You found out what was inside them," Winnie spat.

Olsen paused about halfway up the arch. He grimaced. "Winslow, for the last time, you're not making any sense. What's inside them?"

Winnie's gloved finger danced over the trigger. His breath came hot and fast under the face mask. He knew that Olsen had the advantage here. As long as he kept denying that he knew the truth about the trophies, there was nothing Winnie could do. Winnie couldn't *kill* the old guy, not in his own home. Olsen was so damn cunning. He could always make a person forget how smart he really was, precisely because he acted so stupid. The supposed plot to kidnap Mackenzie was a prime example. That was idiocy worthy of Burwell. But Winnie had bought it. Olsen had suckered him, just the way——

"Give me that gun!"

Suddenly Olsen was diving at Winnie's legs, knocking him to the floor again. The gun flew from his hands. It clattered across the front hall. His brain seemed to fill with smog. For the first time in his life, he couldn't compartmentalize or focus. Everything turned to gray smoke. Panic seized him. So he gave in to it. He had no choice. He staggered to the front door and threw it open, sprinting out into the cold October night.

"Get back here!" Olsen shouted. "Don't you dare think about going to the cops!"

Winnie dashed for the woods. He had no idea where he was headed; he only knew he had to run. But Olsen didn't have to worry. He had no intention of going to *anybody*. Without any evidence, he would only incriminate himself. He'd never been so humiliated. That crafty old man had beaten him. It was a dark, dark moment. The darkest.

The predator had become the prey.

Sunday's letter to her parents

Dear Mom and Dad,

   I'm sure that by now Headmaster Olsen has called you and asked you if you knew where I was or what was going on. I just want you to know that I am safe. I can't really tell you any more than that. I want you to know something else, too. All those times I seemed bored or fed up for no reason at all, or said something sarcastic, or criticized Dad's Goose Hunting Club . . . well, I'm sorry for all that. I was just being bitchy because I was too scared to say what was really on my mind. I was too scared to admit that I felt I had no choices, that my entire life was planned out for me, down to how a certain brand of shoes <u>had</u> to match a certain color barrette at an outdoor midsummer function.

   I don't feel that way anymore, though. And this is going to sound very Hallmark Channel, but I want to thank you for everything you've done and did and will do.

   And one more thing: I know I've complained a lot about Wessex in a passive-aggressive way. (At least, that's what Noah says I've done.) But

I see now that it really isn't such a bad place. It's really just a pretty New England boarding school with a long tradition of turning very privileged children into wonderful, responsible adults. Like you guys.

Love,
Sunday

10

"You know what's so cool?"

Sunday stared blearily at Mackenzie from behind
Hobson's turntables. *No.* She couldn't possibly
imagine what was "cool." Sneaking out of Reed Hall
to spend the night in Hobson's room certainly
didn't qualify. (Especially since his room belonged
in a "Truly Tasteless" episode of MTV's "Cribs.")
Sneaking out *period* didn't qualify, which was kind of
amusing—considering that about two weeks ago,
Sunday had thought that sneaking out was about the
coolest thing in the world. Now she was just sick of
it. All she wanted was a good night's sleep in her
own bed. She could even deal with the Sven Larsen
decor. Anything. Just as long as she could close her
eyes and feel safe . . .

Obviously, though, the triple was the *last* place they could feel safe. They had to stay on the move. No sleep. No fixed location. They had to keep clear of Winnie and Olsen until Noah had given Sal the money. Too much was at stake. (Meaning their lives, although it was best not to think of it in such stark terms.) There was no telling what Winnie or Olsen might do. They were a desperate pair. Not to mention loony tunes. And probably capable of murder. A winning combination, all around.

"Well?" Mackenzie asked, glancing around the room. "Do you?"

"No," Allison grumbled.

The poor girl. Sunday felt genuinely sorry for her. She really did. Given the lack of chairs, Allison had ended up sitting next to Hobson on his bed. *Her ex-boyfriend's bed.* With Mackenzie in the room. It was just . . . ugly. There was no other word for it.

"What's cool, Mack?" Hobson asked.

"That we're all friends again!"

Sunday looked at Allison and Hobson. They both buried their faces in their hands at the exact same time.

"What?" Mackenzie asked. She seemed puzzled. "You don't think all this excitement and running around is bringing us all back together?"

Allison glanced up at her. "You fooled around

with Hobson behind my back," she said flatly. "I think you're jumping the gun a little bit."

"I am?" Mackenzie said.

Sunday cringed. What a pleasant conversation to be having at four in the morning. Of course, she should have figured that they'd get around to this, sooner or later. How could they not? And she supposed she should look at the positives. At the very least, Allison had finally snapped out of her perpetual state of Denial—with a capital *D*. She was finally accepting reality: Hobson had dumped her, Olsen and Winnie were crooks, and life could not be broken down into a Seven-Part Plan. The only problem was that Denial appeared to be contagious, and Mackenzie had come down with a severe case of it.

"Whatever," Mackenzie murmured. "I didn't mean to hurt you."

"Oh, right," Allison said. "I'm just supposed to believe that. I'm just supposed to accept what you wrote in that stupid note, that you and Hobson got together because—"

"Yo, everybody just chill, all right?" Hobson interrupted. "I'm here. I'm in the room. You don't have to talk about me like I'm not. I can hear you."

Allison sighed loudly, then flopped back against the leopard-skin comforter. She closed her eyes and curled up into a little ball. "Forget it. I'm done talking. I'm going to sleep. Wake me up when Fred gets here."

Mackenzie opened her mouth, then closed it.

Sunday hung her head. Ah, yes. This was what being friends was all about. Running around, sharing excitement, sharing the same boyfriend, et cetera . . . all these special bonding experiences. She glanced at the clock on Hobson's wall—a neon Rockette, whose kicking legs were the minute and hour hands. It was later than four. In fact, it was almost five. Where *was* Fred, anyway? He'd told them that he'd needed to catch up on some homework, and that he'd be running a little late.

Homework.

That was almost funny. Sunday hadn't thought about homework in a long, long time.

Actually, it wasn't funny at all. It was extremely stupid. This was fall term senior year, the time when grades counted most. At this point, she'd be lucky to get a D average. Oh, well. *Apex Technical, here I come!* Or maybe she'd just skip college altogether. Or maybe her parents would give some Ivy League institution a six-figure donation, and Sunday wouldn't have to worry about a thing. Membership had its privileges, after all, right? She wondered if Hobson had any Pepto-Bismol. Actually, what she really wondered was how Noah was doing. They hadn't heard so much as a peep from him.

"So," Mackenzie said. "Does anybody want a tarot reading?"

"Mack-*en*-zie," Sunday groaned.

"Baby, this is not the time for freakiness," Hobson mumbled. "I know you're just—"

"Baby?" Allison snapped. "Mackenzie is your *baby* now?"

Somebody knocked softly on the door.

Thank God, Sunday thought.

Hobson jumped up. "Fred?" he whispered.

"Yeah. It's me."

"One sec." Hobson unlocked the latch and let Fred inside. "Anybody see you come here?" he whispered.

Fred shook his head. "No." He flashed Sunday a tired smile. "Hey."

"Hey," she said. She smiled back, but she couldn't help but be a little worried. He looked even more exhausted than usual. He was filthy, too. His jeans and sweatshirt were covered in dirt, and that weird Guatemalan hippie sash he still insisted on wearing had been torn. Of course, that might be a good thing. Maybe now he'd finally get rid of it.

"Are you all right?" Mackenzie asked.

Fred nodded. He looked for a place to sit and finally just plopped down on the floor. "Yeah, I'm fine."

Allison sat up straight. "What happened to you? Did you fall?"

"No. I followed Winnie around tonight."

Sunday jerked. She practically fell off her chair. "You *what*?" she cried.

"Shh!" Hobson whispered. "We gotta chill, yo. Mr. Wendt is a light sleeper."

Fred shrugged. "I'm sorry I didn't tell you, but I knew you wouldn't want me to go. I had to see what he was up to, though. I knew there was no way he'd sit back and let us take his money without a fight. And I know he wouldn't let Olsen screw him. So I trailed him. He didn't see me or anything—"

"Okay, okay, okay," Sunday interrupted, with an odd mix of anger and relief. "We have to make a new rule, all right? No more secrets. No more sneaking around behind each other's backs. Everybody has to know every part of the plan."

"Continuously, at all times," Hobson and Mackenzie added in unison. They smiled at each other.

Allison rolled her eyes.

Fred glanced at Sunday, confused.

"It's a Burwellism," Sunday explained. "He said it . . . a long time ago." The last words stuck in her throat. A wave of guilt swept over her. Hobson and Mackenzie must have felt it, too, because they stopped smiling. It wasn't right to make fun of the guy after he had died, even if he *was* a big fat fool. In the end, he'd just been a victim.

"I'm sorry," Fred said.

"So wassup, yo?" Hobson asked. "What did Winnie do?"

"He dressed up in a ninja outfit and broke into Olsen's house."

Sunday blinked. "A ninja outfit?"

"I guess he was trying to be sneaky or something," Fred said. "But that's not the weirdest part. Olsen must have heard him come in, because he came downstairs and pulled a gun on him." He paused, staring into space. "You know, the gun looked like a toy. I mean, Sal's gun was, like, twice as big. Anyway, I was hiding in the bushes out front, and I saw the whole thing. Winnie attacked him and got the gun. He wanted to know where something called the O.T.C. trophies were. Then Olsen attacked *him* and got the gun back. Then Winnie took off. I waited until Olsen went back to bed, then I came here."

The room was quiet for a moment. All Sunday could think was: *Fred's seen two guns in less than three days. I bet that's more than he ever saw in twelve years of public school.*

"Jesus," Allison finally muttered. "That's insane."

"Word," Hobson said.

Sunday frowned. "I don't get it. The 'O.T.C. trophies'?"

"I don't get it either, if you want to know the truth," Fred said.

"I get it!" Mackenzie exclaimed.

Everybody stared at her.

"Yeah, I get it, too," Hobson said. He bent down and reached under his bed. "I guess since we're not sharing any secrets, I might as well tell you that me and Mack snuck into Olsen's crib. And we found a lot of ill stuff, yo."

Sunday couldn't help but laugh. "*You* guys snuck in there, too? Looks like Fred and I started a trend."

"*I* haven't snuck into Olsen's house," Allison muttered.

Hobson pulled out three cheap-looking trophies and set them down beside Allison on the mattress. "So check it out. 'O.T.C.' One of them has my brother's name on it. For the year 1999. The year he . . ." He hesitated.

"It's okay," Mackenzie said. "You can tell them."

"Tell us what?" Allison asked.

"My brother, Walker . . . see, Olsen set him up. Just the way he set up Noah . . ."

O.T.C. O.T.C. Sunday's mind was whirling. Those initials made perfect sense. She glanced at Fred. "Operation Time Capsule," she said.

Fred nodded. "Yeah. That's just what I was thinking." He pushed himself off the floor and picked up one of the trophies, examining its wide, faux-mahogany base. The bottom was made of black plastic. "Winnie said that there was something hidden inside them. He thought Olsen found out what it was . . ." His eyes narrowed. He poked at something on the plastic, digging his finger into a little indentation. There was a click, and the entire bottom fell open, swinging on a hinge, just like a trapdoor.

Something tumbled out onto the rug.

"Oh my God," they all gasped at once.

It was a computer disk.

"Whoa," Hobson whispered. He bent over and picked it up. "O.T.C. Nineteen ninety-eight," he read from the label. "And it's IBM compatible. Just the way I like 'em." He marched over to his desk and pulled a sleek-looking black laptop out of the top drawer. "Let's open this baby up, yo."

"This is so cool!" Mackenzie squealed. "I mean, I feel like we're in *Charlie's Angels* or something. Isn't this cool? Secret compartments in trophies and ninja outfits—" She paused. "Sorry. I'll shut up now."

Easy there. Sunday patted Mackenzie's shoulder. But she had to admit, she was more than a little excited, herself. Even Allison seemed to forget her grumpiness. They all huddled around Hobson as he opened up the computer and shoved the disk inside. He clicked the mouse a couple of times.

"All right, let's see . . . there are two Word files," he said. "'Affidavit' and 'Breakdown.' Let's start with the—"

Bee-bee-bee-beep!

Everyone flinched.

Sunday clutched Mackenzie's arm. "What is that?" she whispered.

"It . . . it's my cell phone," Allison said. Her voice was shaky. "Olsen must be calling me. I . . . um, well, I got that cell phone I wanted—"

Bee-bee-bee-beep!

"Don't answer it," Fred said.

Allison nodded. She yanked it out of her pocket and turned it off. "I'll turn it back on in a couple of minutes and see if he left a message."

Hobson glanced over his shoulder. "You all ready? I'm gonna do this." He clicked twice on the Affidavit file.

———

November 7, 1998

For the record:

My name is Winslow Ellis. I am 14 years old and a freshman at the Wessex Academy. I live primarily at 4 Oneida Drive, Greenwich, Connecticut, 06175, although my family also has residences in New York City, East Hampton, and Paris.

Since the semester began, I have been volunteering as an administrative assistant in Headmaster Phillip Olsen's office. I asked for the job because I believed such an extracurricular activity would look good on my resume, and that it would allow me to share in the behind-the-scenes, day-to-day business of running a boarding school.

It soon came to my attention, however, that the "business" of running the Wessex Academy was much different than I had imagined. While organizing some of Headmaster Olsen's old files—at his request, I might add—I discovered that he has been extorting money from parents and alumni by placing bets with criminals against his own basketball team. Shocked, and frankly disgusted, I told him that I had no choice but to go to the authorities.

Headmaster Olsen assured me that he and his partners would harm my family if I ever did such a thing or if I ever threatened his position in any way. To prove his sincerity, he produced the eyeball of somebody named Newt Greenblatt (Class of '93) who had apparently crossed him. He keeps it in a pickle jar in the bottom drawer of his desk. Fearing for the lives of my loved ones, I told him that I would go along with whatever he wanted. It was then that he recruited me to help him with another evil, illegal activity—one he calls "Operation Time Capsule."

Every year, seniors are asked to write a revealing "anonymous" personal essay, which is supposed to be buried and dug up 25 years later as some kind of ongoing sociological and historical study. In truth, the submissions are hardly anonymous, and Olsen scours them for compromising information that he can use against the students.

This year, he decided to add blackmail to the list of his crimes. He wanted a nest egg, just in case the Wessex basketball should actually win a game, and he needed a large sum to cover his bets. He asked me to go through the submissions and pick one written by the son or daughter of an alumnus. I discovered that Grady Thomas (a third-generation Wessexonian, like myself), wrote about the underground Ecstasy trade that flourished on campus. He admitted to being a major participant. In his essay, he detailed the hypocrisy of the wealthy students who spoke of the campus's "overall lack of morals" while at the same time profiting from drug sales.

While I don't condone the use or sale of drugs, I certainly respected his candor. He never expected anyone to see what he had written until the year 2023.

Olsen arranged for a first-year music teacher, Mr. Timothy Robards (age 22) to purchase 100 tablets of Ecstasy from Grady. Another teacher, Paul Burwell (age 45), who has an enthusiastic interest in filmmaking, videotaped the transaction. This was "Phase One." Olsen used the video to blackmail the Thomas family into paying him $75,000. This was "Phase Two." In the words of the letter he wrote, the sum was "to ensure that evidence of Grady's crimes won't fall into the wrong hands."

We split the money four ways: "Phase Three." I put my own share in an offshore account, the sum total of which I intend to donate to charity.

I only hope that God will forgive me for my collusion with these criminals.

Respectfully submitted,

Winslow Ellis

"I knew it," Sunday breathed. "I *knew* it."

Hobson smirked. "Can you believe this bull? Does he actually think something like this is gonna hold up in court?"

Fred shook his head. "Who knows *what* that guy thinks?"

"Word," Hobson said.

"Do you really think that Olsen keeps somebody's eye in a pickle jar?" Mackenzie asked.

"I'm sure it's a fake," Sunday said. "I think it's a Shakespearean gag. You know, from *Macbeth*. 'Eye of Newt.' Anyway, let's print this thing out."

"I don't have a printer, yo," Hobson said. "We have to go to the computer center."

"It's five in the morning," Allison pointed out. "All the buildings are closed." She turned her cell phone back on and held it up to her ear. "I have a message, by the way."

She swallowed. "It's Olsen—he wants to know if I've seen Winnie. . . . He says that Winnie tried to break into his house tonight. . . . He's walking around campus, looking for him."

Hobson popped the disk out of his laptop and closed it. "Damn," he said. "We should get out of here."

Sunday nodded. Her heart bounced in her chest. Winnie lived on the first floor. Olsen would probably check his room first. It wouldn't be long after that before he came knocking on Hobson's door. In a flash, all five of them were scrambling for the trophies, their coats, their shoes—anything they could possibly grab.

"Where should we go?" Allison whispered. She looked pale.

"We should get off campus," Fred said. "We should hide out somewhere in New Farmington—near the train station, so we can be there when Noah gets back. . . ."

For some reason, Hobson dove under the bed again.

"What are you doing?" Sunday hissed.

"I found something else in Olsen's basement, too," he grunted. He squirmed back out with the miniature treasure chest.

Sunday stared at it. She remembered it from Olsen's trophy case. Mostly, she remembered that it looked like the kind of cheesy souvenir a father would buy his 5-year-old on a business trip. "What is that?" she asked.

"I don't know," Hobson said. "It's locked. But if we found disks in those trophies . . ."

"I'll open it," Fred said, reaching for the door. "I'm an expert at picking locks."

Sunday raised her eyebrows at him.

He paused as the rest of them filed quietly out into the hall. "Well," he mumbled after a moment. "Maybe not an *expert*."

Postcard sent to Charles Percy from the Cayman Islands

10/24

Dear Dad,

How are you? I'm doing <u>great</u>. I promised you a postcard, remember? Anyway, I'm at the airport right now, on my way back to the States. The Caymans were more beautiful than I ever imagined. Unfortunately, I couldn't go scuba diving because you're not supposed to scuba dive and fly on the same day. Oh, well. Win a few, lose a few. So now it's off to Quogue to bargain with the Mafia. Wish me luck!

Love,
Noah

P.S. You can forget that philosophical question I asked you in the last letter. I got it all figured out.

P.P.S. But don't forget the stuff about the "big bucks" funeral. I meant all that.

11

If there had been any doubt in Noah's mind that crime did indeed pay (and pay well), it vanished the moment his cab turned onto Stone Hill Terrace. It was a dead end, and there was only one residence. And actually, *residence* was not the most appropriate word. *Compound* was closer. *Dark Fortress of Evil* was probably dead on the mark, but Noah didn't want to jump the gun until he'd actually been inside. Unfortunately, he couldn't see much of the house from the street. The entire place was surrounded by a ten-foot-high brick wall.

"So here we are," the cab driver grunted, pulling up to the curb. Unlike Noah's cab driver in the Caymans, this guy was neither a prophet nor a mystic—just a grizzled old man named Ryan McSwiggan.

His cab stank of cigars. (Or maybe he *was* a mystic. Who could tell anymore?) He punched the meter. "That'll be sixty-five bucks."

Noah glanced at his watch. It was eleven-fifteen. He still had forty-five minutes until the deadline. *Thank God.* He hadn't been sure he would make it. His plane had been delayed, and he'd thought it would take at least two hours to get from JFK to Quogue. Luckily, Mr. McSwiggan didn't seem to be acquainted with any traffic laws—

"Excuse me? Kid? Are you deaf? *Sixty-five bucks.*"

"Oh. Yeah. Sorry." Noah dug his wallet out of the inside pocket of his seersucker suit. "Hey look, can I ask you a favor?"

Mr. McSwiggan glared at him in the rearview mirror.

"I'm gonna give you a hundred," Noah said. "There's another hundred in it for you if you wait for me out here and take me back to New York. Okay?"

"How long you gonna be?"

"Not longer than twenty minutes. Any longer than that, you can take off, and the hundred is yours. But if that happens . . . well, never mind."

"Two hundred bucks, huh? You got yourself a deal."

"Great. Thanks." Noah pulled a crisp hundred out of his wallet—a cash advance on his credit card, which, miraculously, his father hadn't canceled—and handed it over. "I'll be right back." He grabbed his briefcase and hopped out onto the sidewalk. "Now, remember—"

"So long, jerk-ass!" Mr. McSwiggan yelled. He gunned the engine and spun the car around with a deafening screech, then sped away in a cloud of exhaust.

Noah watched him go.

"Great," he said. "So you just wait here. I'll be right back."

The roar of the engine faded.

I really should have had some free mimosas on the flight.

Noah glanced at the brick wall. At the far end, there was a forbidding iron gate with a buzzer. He started toward it. He suddenly realized that this might not even *be* the Viverito residence. Maybe they'd moved since the last update of the alumni directory.

No, they lived here. The mailbox was marked VIVERITO. Not a lot of gray area there.

So. This was it. So much for wishful thinking. Noah pressed the buzzer.

After a couple of seconds, static burst from the speaker.

"Yeah?" somebody barked.

"Salvatore?"

"No. Tony."

"Oh, hey, Tony," Noah said. He smiled, then

realized he was talking to a plastic box. "It's Noah Per—I mean, it's—you know, it's—"

"I know who you are."

The gates clicked, then slowly parted.

Noah stared at the swinging iron doors. His knees wobbled. Now that he could see the house, he realized that it *was*, in fact, a Dark Fortress of Evil. It was one of those stark, Scandinavian, neo-ultra-postmodern jobs—all gray wood with broad, symmetrical rows of tinted black windows on weird turrets and boxlike wings. He forced himself to march across the gravel driveway to the front door. His feet crunched on the stones. He wondered if any people were buried out here. Nah . . . probably not. It was too close to home.

The front door opened just as he reached for it.

Tony stood in the front hall. He was wearing blue nylon jogging pants and no shirt. It looked as if he'd put on a little weight in the weeks since he'd been expelled. A flabby paunch hung over his waistband.

"We just got PlayStation Two," he said.

"Oh." Noah smiled again. "Congratulations."

Tony's face was blank. He turned and walked back into the house, leaving the door open.

"So . . . uh, I guess I'll just come in, then," Noah said.

He glanced over his shoulder. The iron gates had swung shut. There was no escape.

Just go in there and give them the money, he said to himself. He took a deep breath. Then he took another. He had to approach this from a businessman's perspective. He had to be Winslow Ellis again—or at least he had to think the way Winnie thought. He had to think like a high roller. He was walking into a house with close to two hundred thousand dollars. He had no weapons, no boxing or martial arts skills, no muscle tone to speak of. What he did have was an enormous capacity to annoy people. And speaking of the money, he was also thirteen thousand dollars short of the appointed sum. How easy would it be for Sal to pump a bullet into his puny chest—*thwip!*—then pocket the check and take Noah for a "diving lesson" in the Atlantic Ocean?

It would be quite easy. It was hard to think of anything that would be easier.

"Ohh!" a voice yelled from deep inside the house. "Did you see that pass? Am I Tom Brady or what? Look at me! Worship me!"

"Eat me," another voice said.

Noah couldn't tell if the voices belonged to Sal and Tony. Maybe they belonged to some other ultraviolent felon.

Well, at the very least, he should take stock of what was truly important here: He wasn't going to die a virgin. In fact, he should be grateful. Most people didn't experience the same kind of good fortune in the last days of their lives. At seventeen (a not-quite-attractive, occasionally pimply, and highly insecure seventeen at that), he'd slept with not one, but *two* women. Not girls, either. *Women.* Twenty-two-year-olds. He should have told his father he wanted *that* inscribed on the giant toilet-bowl tombstone. It was by far his proudest achievement.

He walked through the door.

The interior had a very simple, picture-gallery theme, centered entirely around sports. The white walls were adorned with framed posters of famous athletes, past and present, all autographed with magic marker. Most were action shots. Dunks, catches, goals. Lots of sweating and outstretched tongues. He recognized some of the people on the wall: Joe Namath, Michael Jordan, O.J. Simpson (*O.J. Simpson?*), that hockey player guy. . . . Where did the Viveritos sit, though? There weren't any chairs.

"Touchdown!" somebody shouted. "In your face!"

Noah followed the voice around a corner into a vast living-room area. The ceiling was twenty feet high, at least. It was unfurnished except for wall-to-wall white carpet, a TV the size of a small car, and a sloppy pile of video game cartridges.

Sal and Tony were there. They sat side by side,

less than four feet from the screen. Both were furiously wrestling with a pair of joysticks. Neither was wearing a shirt. Sal was even pudgier than his brother.

"You suck," Sal said.

"No, *you* suck," Tony said.

"It would be hard to suck worse than you," Sal said.

"Then why do you have the word *sucker* tattooed on your forehead?"

"You take sucking to a new level," Sal said. "See? Game over. Ha!" He scrambled forward and punched the power button. The screen winked off.

Tony exhaled deeply, then dropped the joystick. "You suck the most," he said.

Sal glanced up at Noah. "Thirsty?" he asked.

"Uh . . . yeah, actually," Noah said. He clutched the briefcase in front of him, gripping the handle with both hands. "Thanks."

"Go get us some Cokes, Tony," Sal said.

Tony nodded. He pushed himself off the floor and left without a word.

"I hope Coke is okay," Sal said. "It's all we got."

Noah shrugged. "Coke is fine."

"You got a problem, Noah."

"I do?" He smiled. *Please don't let me faint right now.*

Sal's eyes flashed to the rug. "Have a seat."

"Um . . . okay." Noah sat cross-legged on the rug. He didn't let go of the briefcase.

"Your problem is low self-esteem. The last time we met, you told me that you hated somebody named Noah Percy, and that you were happy he was in Tibet. But you were right there in the room with me. If that doesn't smack of low self-esteem, I don't know what does."

Noah tried to keep his eyes from wandering to Sal's bare gut. "Oh. That was just a joke." He forced a laugh. "I joke around when I get nervous."

"Lots of people do," Sal said. "It's a common defense mechanism."

"That's true," Noah agreed. Something was bothering him—but it wasn't until Sal had said the words *defense mechanism* that he could put his finger on it. "Hey, can I ask you a personal question? It might offend you."

Sal shrugged. "Try me. What's the worst that can happen?"

"What happened to your Long Island accent? You sound like my Uncle Adrian. He grew up on Madison Avenue."

"We'll get to that in a bit. I like your suit, by the way." Sal nodded at the briefcase. "You can open that any time you want."

Noah laughed again. "Oh, right." He fumbled with the clasps. His fingers were moist. After several attempts, he finally managed to get the briefcase open. He spun it around so that it was facing Sal. "Here you go. It's all yours."

Sal peered inside. "Let's see . . . a pair of underwear, some deodorant—"

"The check's in the front pocket," Noah said quickly.

"Let's take a look, then." He reached inside and pulled out the slip of paper. He studied it for a moment, his face stony. "One hundred eighty-seven thousand, four hundred and four dollars, U.S., payable to Winslow Ellis," he read. "Interesting." He glanced up at Noah. "Tell me. What am I supposed to do with this?"

Noah swallowed. This sounded like a trick question. "Deposit it?" he guessed.

"My name's not Winslow Ellis," he said.

"I endorsed it to you." He pointed a shaky finger at the back.

"Your name's not— Relax, Noah." He grinned. "Your name's not Winslow Ellis, either."

"I forged his signature. It's a spot-on match. Look at it. Go ahead and flip the check over. 'Pay to the order of Salvatore Viverito.' I practiced a bunch of times. Hundreds. I know it as well as I know my own. His family has been sending my family Christmas cards since we were kids, and he always signed them. Listen, I asked the woman at the bank to give me cash, but she—"

"Relax, relax, okay?" Sal murmured. "It's fine. No problem."

Noah blinked. It was a little difficult to relax, seeing as his heart was doing an unrequested, frenzied, out-of-time drum solo. "Fine?" he choked out.

"Okay, 'fine' might be an exaggeration. The figure is a little less than two—"

"I'll get you the rest," Noah promised. "I can withdraw up to twenty thousand dollars in cash on my dad's credit card."

Sal chuckled. "Nah. I'm kidding. This is great."

"Really?"

"Yeah. You look unhappy."

"No, no, it's just . . ." Gradually, Noah's heart settled into a steady, rapid, techno-style beat: *thump-thump-thump* . . . "I mean, I didn't know the—well, you know, the people in your line of work—I, uh—"

"You didn't think that the Mafia could be so accommodating?"

Noah nodded. "Something like that," he said. "I was just looking for a more politically correct term than *Mafia*."

"Is there one?"

"I don't know. *Cosa Nostra?*"

"Let me tell you a little story, Noah."

Just then, Tony reappeared with two Cokes. He handed one to Noah. The can was warm. Noah didn't care. He popped it open and guzzled the room-temperature fizz, nearly gagging. Tony gave the other one to Sal, then left again.

Sal placed the Coke at his side without opening it. He stood up and walked over to the row of windows. "Do you know my girlfriend, Diane?" he asked, scratching his belly.

Noah shook his head. "No. I've heard about her, though."

"From Fred Wright?" Sal glanced over his shoulder.

"Yeah."

"What did he say about her?"

"Not a whole lot. Mostly that he was pissed at her."

Sal nodded. "Yeah. That figures. You know, I kind of feel sorry for the kid. He never had a chance with her. It was a bad time for us, and we drifted apart. But I always knew she'd come back. See, Diane and I grew up together. Our families live in the same building in the city. I mean, that's where my dad spends most of his time. He cleared this house out a long time ago; it's pretty much just a crash pad for Tony and me. Anyway, Diane and I fell in love in the ninth grade. It was right out of a movie. I fell in love with the girl next door. Or close enough. She was on twelve; I was on eight.

Anyway, I went to Wessex. She went to Carnegie Mansion. But I was able to sign out and visit her on the weekends. My dad was always totally cool about giving me permission to leave. . . ."

Noah desperately tried to concentrate on what Sal was saying, but he couldn't. All he could think about was the Sal Viverito he remembered from two years before—the one who hung out with Carlton Douglas, the one who was cocky and aloof (as all seniors were, especially around sophomores), who wore a baseball cap, who listened to the Dave Matthews Band . . . to cut to the chase, the one who acted like a typical Long Island meathead. And yes, fine, Noah stereotyped people. Life was more efficient that way. Or it *had* been until now, anyway. That was the problem: the old Sal and this Sal had absolutely nothing in common, except an exceptionally casual wardrobe. Where was the talk? (As in "tawk.") Where were the threats, the guns, the maniacal laughter? Noah shouldn't be drinking warm Coke right now; he should be tied to a chair while Sal wolfed down forkfuls of ravioli.

". . . The point is, she's a hippie at heart, Noah. She would *never* go out with a Mafia guy. Do you understand?"

"No," Noah said. "No, I don't understand at all. Not one bit."

Sal frowned at him. "Well, let me put it to you this way. Would you say that boarding schools are generally places where kids reinvent themselves?"

A vision of Hobson appeared in Noah's mind—standing behind the microphone at a dance and rapping along to "Real Slim Shady," wearing a leather Wu Wear jacket so big that it looked almost like a vampire's cape.

"I guess so," Noah said.

"Right," Sal said. "And I was one of those kids. Maybe you were, too. I was shy. I read a lot. Wasn't good at sports, didn't play an instrument—but my father, see, my father was a tough guy. Steakhouses, the tracks, that kind of thing. Some people even thought he was connected, and he got a huge kick out of that—"

"I'm sorry," Noah interrupted. "They *thought* he was connected? Isn't—"

"Just let me finish. So I come to Wessex, right? I'm a freshman, and I decide, what the hell? Nobody knows me here. I can be a tough guy, too. *I* can be connected." He slipped back into the accent for a second. "You know: 'Sal Viverito of da Viverito family.' And Diane is far enough away so that she doesn't have to see me acting this way. I never let her come to Wessex. I always go to visit her at Carnegie Mansion, so she can't see what I'm doing. And when I'm with her, I'm back to being the shy, sensitive guy."

Jesus Christ. The Coke nearly slipped from Noah's fingers. He'd almost forgotten he was holding it. One thing was for sure: His mind was in no danger of wandering anymore. Sal had captured his attention now. Oh, yes. He was riveted. He was more than riveted. He was practically panting, like a starving dog at mealtime.

"So, the thing is, the more I act this way, the more natural it becomes," Sal went on. "It almost stops *being* an act. It's like, I can't separate the real me from this new, phony me. I start getting really into reading about the Mob, seeing all the old movies—all of it. And people buy it, Noah. They buy it. I mean, take the stuff about giving you a 'diving lesson.' That crap just comes to me. Pretty good, huh?"

Noah nodded. No argument there. The gun had helped, of course.

"Anyway, right about Christmastime freshman year, right when the basketball season is about to start, Olsen calls me into his office. He makes up a bunch of bull about how I violated the rules about leaving campus without permission. He says, 'How would your father like it if we suspended you?' Then he starts asking me about my father. Says he hears that Carmine Viverito is a pretty impressive guy. Knows the right people, eats at the right restaurants, all that crap. Then he starts asking me if me or my dad know anything about basketball. Or betting. He says maybe we can come to some kind of agreement if I help him out with some business."

"Olsen approached *you*?" Noah gasped.

Sal smiled. "And I went with it. I mean, I freaking *rolled* with it, man. Right there, sitting in Olsen's office, with that goddamn Shakespeare statue—I don't know what the hell got into me. The stuff just started coming out of my mouth. I say, yeah, I can place bets, but to deal with the people I deal with, you got to lay out five Gs, minimum. Olsen says that's no problem. He's got a pool of guys, just waiting to drop loads of cash. So I run the show myself, calling in the bets, and the next thing I know, I'm making thousands. On prep school basketball."

That was it. Noah dropped the Coke. It wasn't even so much the shock of Sal's confession. It was more that Noah could relate to it. *He'd* been in that same situation, too: sitting in Olsen's chair, just going off on whatever popped into his head. . . . But that was a conversation for another time. There was a bubbly, caramel-colored stain spreading across the rug. He jumped up and searched frantically for anything to clean it up with.

"Don't worry," Sal said. "All our rugs are messed up. The maid will handle it. I want to get out of here, anyway. Come on. Follow me. There's something I want to show you."

"You sure?" Noah asked. "I'm really, really sorry—"

"Yeah, I'm sure. Come on." He beckoned Noah out into the hall. "It'll only take a minute."

For the merest fraction of a second, Noah hesitated. He was in the guy's home. He'd just ruined a rug. He couldn't escape. There was no point in protesting, though. And as he followed Sal back past all the posters, he realized that there was one big piece missing from Sal's story—if he'd even understood the story correctly. Two big pieces, really: Miss Burke and Mr. Burwell. If what Sal was saying was true, if he really *wasn't* in the Mafia (although he still hadn't spelled it out in such specific terms—which was evidence of an understanding of the law, a talent shared by all Mafiosi) . . . then why had he killed two teachers? What could he possibly have stood to gain from murder? Wasn't that a little . . . gruesome?

Sal paused in front of a door at the end of a long, dark corridor. There was a framed picture of Yogi Berra mounted on it. *To Carmine: All the best. —Yogi.*

"Look, Noah," Sal said with a sigh. "I'm telling you all this because it got out of hand. I've been doing this for six years. I'm getting out of the game.

My little scam ended up affecting my relationships. Diane started to notice this double life I was leading, and she thought I was a hypocrite and a fake, and so I had to give it up. And when I realized Olsen and the other one—the fat kid, Winnie—were such schizoids . . . I knew enough was enough. I mean, I'm not a violent guy. That stuff with the gun at your friend's house—I'm sorry about that. Really. And those were just BBs, by the way. The point is, this whole thing has gone on way too long. It's over. It's time to get on with my life."

Noah nodded, mostly because he figured that was the safest thing to do. If anybody was a "schizoid," it was clearly Sal. He sounded as if he'd rehearsed that soliloquy for an afternoon talk show: *Today on "Ricki Lake": Six Years of Pretending to be a Mobster are Finally Catching Up with Me!* In all probability, Sal was just trying to put Noah at ease before he yanked out the pistol and whacked him. In fact, this was probably the "whacking room."

Sal opened the door.

Noah found himself looking at Miss Burke and Mr. Burwell.

They were sitting on narrow twin beds with packed suitcases beside them. Miss Burke's hair was in a ponytail. She was wearing a floral print dress. Mr. Burwell had a couple of days' worth of beard growth on his face. Today's double-breasted suit was navy blue.

Okay . . .

This was . . . not expected.

Think, Noah. Think. The way he figured it, there were two plausible explanations. (1) Tony had spiked his soda with a very powerful dose of PCP, or (2) the Viverito family had perfected the art of hologram presentation. Actually, there could be a third: These could be imposters wearing those *Mission Impossible*-style rubber masks. Noah pondered all three for a moment. Well, actually, given the realism of the scene, none of these explanations was likely. He imagined it would be hard to reproduce the exact folds in Burwell's double chin, even given current special-effects technology. And Burwell (or whoever he was) definitely wasn't dead. Neither was Miss Burke. They looked far too healthy for a pair of mangled corpses—maybe a little tired, but definitely breathing.

"It's safe for you to go now," Sal said.

They both nodded.

Noah blinked a few times. He could feel a very large lump forming in his throat. He wasn't the crying sort, but all at once he felt like bursting into tears. He'd experienced a lot of shocking things in the past few days—some of which he'd prayed to the

Almighty he'd never see again, others of which had made him feel like a rock star on a wild romp at the Playboy Mansion—but this . . . he couldn't articulate what was going through his head. For once in his life, he was too overwhelmed to start babbling.

"I don't get it," he choked out. "What happened?"

"Mr. Burwell called me on Saturday," Sal said. "He said that Olsen and Winnie were ripping him off, and he wanted to know if I was in on it. When he told me what was up, I figured it would be best if I got involved. I knew the old man was planning something bad."

"But Fred and Sunday saw them go into the quarry!" Noah yelled. He was almost afraid to look at them, as if they were ghosts. Maybe they *were* ghosts. "Fred and Sunday saw them in the car, and they saw the car—"

"Dude, chill," Sal said, laughing. "Just take it easy, all right? Everything's okay."

Noah was starting to hyperventilate.

"Salvatore saved my life," Miss Burke said solemnly.

"Mine, too," Burwell added.

It was *their* voices. It was *them*.

"It was no big deal," Sal said. "It was all a show for Olsen. I knew he was there, hiding out. The whole thing was a setup. He asked Mr. Burwell to get rid of Miss Burke at the quarry. He was planning a hit. He was gonna wait and kill both of them himself. So I beat him to it." He laughed. "Although these two *were* a little freaked when I came screeching up behind them. They didn't know who to trust."

Noah shook his head. "So the whole thing was fake?"

Sal nodded, beaming. "A work of art, if I do say so myself. And the best part is Olsen thinks I whacked them to scare *him*. So now Tony gets to go back to school."

"He deserves to go to school," Burwell said quietly. He turned to Noah. His beady eyes were rheumy—but whether that was due to a swelling of emotion, or exhaustion, or maybe just a lot of beer, Noah wasn't sure. "I was the one who set him up. I deserved to be punished. And I should apologize to you, too, Percy. You were always a stand-up kid. Aside from the toilet thing, your behavior was always very demonstrable. You were just a wise-ass. You know, calling me 'Dad' and crap like that."

Noah tried to smile. *Demonstrable?*

"I was frustrated," Burwell added. "With everything. Twenty years at that school, you know? Same old same old—day in and day out. Teaching you trust fund kids, with your houses and your swimming pools, and I . . . well, I just wanted a piece of the action. I never thought anybody would get hurt. I mean, *really* hurt. You and Tony were the first kids who actually got kicked out. But I . . . I had a dream, see. I was gonna take my share and split. I was gonna write my screenplay. And then I was gonna give my share back to the people I took it from."

"Maybe you still can," Noah said.

"Yeah." Burwell laughed grimly. "Maybe."

"Hey, what did I tell you?" Sal said. "My buddy Carlton's dad owns Paramount. Or something like that."

"Noah, I owe you an apology, too," Miss Burke said. Her voice was strained. "I—"

"Hey, hey," Sal said. "Enough already. This is something you two should discuss in private. Come on. Let's get out of here."

Miss Burke and Mr. Burwell reached for their bags.

Noah glanced at Sal. "Where are we going?"

"Back to Wessex," Sal said. "I gotta drive Tony up there so he can have time to get settled in and get ready for classes tomorrow." He jerked his head toward Mr. Burwell and Miss Burke. "And these guys gotta get back to teaching."

"Whoa, wait a second," Noah said. He almost laughed. "Get back to *teaching*? What about Olsen and Winnie?"

Sal smirked. "We'll figure something out." He patted Noah on the back. "Nice job on the money, by the way. I didn't think you'd be able to pull that off."

"Neither did I. Hey, Sal, can I ask you a question?"

"Sure."

"What does your father *do*, anyway?"

Sal shrugged. "Nothing, really. He's got a trust fund. Just like you." He scratched his bare belly again. "You know, that's probably why so many people think he's mobbed up. He dresses slick, has loads of cash, and spends all day hanging around fancy places and telling all kinds of crazy stories." He burped. "You might want to think about that."

Winslow Ellis's letter to his parents

10/24

DEAR MOM AND DAD,

I DON'T KNOW IF YOU'VE HEARD FROM HEADMASTER OLSEN YET, BUT IF YOU HAVE, IT'S TIME YOU LEARNED THE TRUTH. FOR THE LAST FOUR YEARS, I HAVE BEEN LIVING IN A STATE OF TERROR. YOU THINK OLSEN IS JUST A JOLLY OLD SHAKESPEARE BUFF? HE'S SATAN. HEADMASTER OLSEN HAS COERCED ME INTO COMMITTING TERRIBLE, TERRIBLE CRIMES. THAT WHOLE STOCK-SWINDLING THING LAST YEAR? THAT WAS HIS IDEA. I SWEAR. I DON'T KNOW ANYTHING ABOUT THE STOCK MARKET!

APPARENTLY, HE WANTS TO GET RID OF ME BECAUSE HE THINKS I KNOW TOO MUCH. HE'S FABRICATED ALL KINDS OF ELABORATE EVIDENCE THAT SUPPOSEDLY "PROVES" I BLACK-MAILED A BUNCH OF STUDENTS. I NEVER KEPT A CENT! HE'S CONNECTED WITH THE MAFIA. HE FORCED ME TO SELL TOBACCO TO KIDS AND TOOK ALL THE MONEY. HE BOUGHT ALL THE NOTEBOOKS IN THE SCHOOL STORE AND SOLD THEM BACK TO THE STUDENTS AT A PROFIT. HE STASHED $187,404.00 IN A CAYMAN ISLANDS BANK ACCOUNT. HE THREW THE CARNEGIE MANSION EXHIBITION GAME ON PURPOSE. HE ADMITTED FRED WRIGHT AS A POSTGRAD, EVEN THOUGH FRED READS AT THE FIFTH-GRADE LEVEL. HE TRICKED NOAH PERCY INTO HAVING SEX WITH A TEACHER, MISS BURKE. THEN HE KILLED HER. HE killed Mr. Burwell, too. I know where the bodies are. He sold marijuana to Walker Crowe. He used school funds to pay for his own custom Nerf basketball court, trophy case, and trophies.

I need help. Please notarize this letter.

Your loving son,
Winnie

Part V
The Harvest Ball

12

Winnie knew he couldn't hide out forever at the New Farmington post office. Coming here might have been foolish. It was bad form to regret any move. . . . Still, maybe he should have just stayed at the Waldorf, where he'd spent the rest of the night and most of the day.

He could have just *called* his parents.

But, no, the letter had been smart. He'd done the right thing. Phone calls were temporal: here, then gone. You couldn't *hold* a phone call. A letter was solid. Anything solid could be used as a weapon—or as an exhibit to be displayed at trial, should the need ever arise. Letters also had a whole sort of anguished, "I-can't-get-to-the-phone-because-I'm-too-scared" air of desperation about them. That was the subtext, anyway.

Not that he had to put much effort into it, given his current situation. But anything helped.

He hurried out of the post office and back down South Chapel Street toward campus. The sidewalk was strewn with dead leaves. He kicked them. What a mess. Somebody should come out here with a goddamn rake. Weren't there any public sanitation workers in New Farmington? Everybody always talked about how *beautiful* this town was in the fall, how *picturesque*. And he'd agreed. Oh, yes—a town like New Farmington is a dying breed, he'd told Mackenzie's mother . . . when had it been? At some alumni function last year? Something like that. He'd charmed her with his knowledge of the town's history, its Victorian architecture.

He didn't give a rat's ass about history *or* Victorian architecture.

But he understood something that few others did: A person had to know just enough to *appear* to give a rat's ass. That was all that counted. Most people actually believed in sincerity. The people around here, anyway. Leave the pursuit of wisdom and good conversation to the fools who valued "bettering" themselves (whatever that meant)—that was what Winnie said. Power lay in the subtle science of knowing how to react to others, how to mimic the right moves: the right laugh, the right glance, the right handshake, the right affectation of interest—anything that conveyed empathy, *understanding*. At their core, people just wanted a connection. Like Allison, for instance. She'd been so lonely and humiliated after Hobson. . . .

Yes, yes. The predators forged those connections. The prey hungered for them.

Although . . . maybe he was wrong to think of himself as a predator. He shook his head as he turned onto Kendall Lane. He'd underestimated his own vulnerability. Dressing up in that Ninja suit, steeling his nerves with the words of mass murderers . . . *Jesus*. It made him wince just to think about it. He knew better than that. Giving himself a label meant giving himself a weakness. He was *beyond* being a predator. He couldn't define what he was. Neither could anyone else. And that was what would give him the edge he needed to survive this mess.

He pushed open the big, Gothic-looking doors of Logan Hall. Screw the label. His truly idiotic mistake had been to stow those disks in those trophies. Yes, he'd backed up all the files on his hard drive—but still, what the hell had he been thinking?

All right. It *had* been a good plan, on its face. A *clever* plan. But perhaps he'd placed too much value on reverse psychology. Perhaps he'd even been brainwashed. He'd read *Bull Your Way Into the Market!*

and *There's a Sucker Bidding Every Minute* cover to cover a dozen times. Those books had made him hundreds of thousands of dollars. And the central lesson of both was the same: Always do what your enemy, partner, or victim least expects.

Olsen should *never* have suspected those disks were in his basement. That was the beauty of Winnie's thinking. If Winnie had moved them—or even if he hadn't—and the police had come knocking on Olsen's door—and they still might—Winnie could have tipped them off to evidence Olsen had "hidden." The plan would have exonerated Winnie and incriminated Olsen at the same time. Winnie could just picture the look on Olsen's face if the cops had stumbled onto the trophies in a closet or bathroom somewhere. He would have had no idea what was going on until the very last second, when the cops opened up the bottoms——

Christ. What now?

A manila envelope was Scotch-taped to his door.

He ripped it off and tore it open. There were several letter-sized papers inside, stapled together in the top right-hand corner. He yanked them out and dropped the envelope on the floor.

Dear Winnie,
    Enclosed is your "affidavit" swearing your innocence in Operation Time Capsule,

as well as the breakdown of the profits for each operation for the past four years. You'll also see that additional affidavits are enclosed: At least twenty students have admitted to purchasing illegal tobacco products, school store items, and beer from you—and they have provided sworn testimony as to exact amounts, dates, and figures.

All told, your offenses will ensure your expulsion, if not prison time. We are also currently working to secure an additional fifty affidavits, and plan to contact the police about your role as an accessory after the fact in the murders of Paul Burwell and Patricia Burke. As an 18-year-old, you will be tried as an adult.

Our demands are as follows:

1) That you withdraw from the Wessex Academy, effective immediately;

2) That you reimburse every person for every item you ever sold to them; and

3) That you help bring Headmaster Phillip Olsen to justice.

Winnie didn't bother to read any further. The gist of the threat was clear. He rolled the pages into a tight cylinder, gripping it until his knuckles whitened. He probably should have taken Fred and Sunday a little more seriously when they'd talked about sneaking in and out of Olsen's house.

Apparently, they hadn't limited themselves to the rolltop desk. They had evidently ventured into the trophy case as well. And now those amateurs actually believed they had Winnie cornered. They believed that *they* could make the demands. With a feeble stack of computer printouts and sworn testimony from known substance abusers.

But they would pay. All of them would pay.

Winnie was sick and tired of running scared. Hiding from Olsen wasn't serving any purpose, either. No. There was only one solution: Destroy everyone and everything.

Right. He would convince Olsen to help him dispose of Sunday, Fred, and whoever else—then *he* would dispose of Olsen. And he would pin everything on Burwell and Burke, just as Olsen had planned to do. Now that those poor fools were dead, they could actually come in pretty handy. And so would the rest of them, when their time came. Because Winnie would be the last one standing. Winnie would be the hero who uncovered the monstrous plot to defile the Wessex Academy.

The lie would become the truth.

Olsen was sitting at his rolltop desk when Winnie burst through the front door. He didn't so much as look up.

Winnie stormed into the living room.

"I assume you got one of these, as well?" Headmaster Olsen asked. He held up an empty manila envelope. His reading glasses were perched on the end of his nose.

Winnie peered over Olsen's shoulder. Sure enough, Olsen was reading the exact same letter that he himself had received. Well, it wasn't *exactly* the same, obviously. Where Winnie's letter had mentioned tobacco, school store items, and beer, Olsen's letter mentioned drugs, pornography, and blackmail. And demand number three was reversed: "That you help bring Winslow Ellis to justice."

"What do you think?" Olsen asked.

"They're trying to turn us against each other," Winnie said.

Olsen sniffed and pushed his glasses up. "Seems like they've already done a good job of that. Where have you been hiding, by the way? I've been searching for you all day."

Winnie shrugged. "Around," he said. "Look, Phil—I mean, Headmaster Olsen, I'm sorry I broke into your house last night. I admit I wanted to protect myself. I don't want to go to jail. I don't want to lose everything I've got. And I know you don't, either. We've worked too hard and come too far to let Sunday Winthrop and Fred Wright ruin everything we've achieved. You know what we have to do. We have to stick together on this. They *want* us to come apart at the seams. If we do that, we'll be playing right into their hands. We have to take care of them: Noah, Allison Scott—and anybody else who might know something. Agreed?"

Olsen didn't answer.

"Agreed?"

"Taking care of them would be sort of a moot point, don't you think?" Olsen mumbled.

Winnie frowned. "Why?"

"Why?" Olsen spat back, glaring up at him. His jowls turned beet red. "Because we had until noon today to get Sal his two hundred thousand dollars, and now it's three-forty-five. Which means that in a matter of minutes, he'll be showing up at my door to take care of *us*."

Once again, that gray smog of panic was creeping into Winnie's brain. He couldn't seem to pin down any one plan, thought, or course of action.

"So . . . so what do you want to do?" he asked.

Olsen's lips twisted. "I've managed to scrape together about fifty thousand. Hopefully that'll convince him to let us live until we can get the rest."

Winnie swallowed. "Do you think we can?"

"I don't know," he muttered. "But I *do* know one thing. We have to turn the tables on these kids.

Think about it. What matters most to all of you? And to your parents?"

How the hell should I know? Winnie thought, glaring back at him. He wasn't in prime shape for the Socratic method right now.

"Your reputations, you fool," Olsen said. "And I have just the thing that will destroy the good names of the Winthrops, the Wildes, the Scotts, the Percys, the Crowes . . . all of them. And believe me, in spite of Chuck Percy's attitude and Travis Crowe's threats, neither wants his name besmirched. Particularly Mortimer. He's involved with illegal gambling. He paid off the school to keep Walker from getting expelled. And both his sons know it." He raised his eyebrows. "One of them even wrote about it."

"The time capsule submissions," Winnie breathed shakily.

Olsen nodded, a cruel smile on his lips. "Safely tucked away. I've got more dirt on more students than even *you* can possibly imagine." He picked up the envelope and waved it in Winnie's face. "So now I'm going to send out my *own* envelope. With my *own* demands. One hundred fifty thousand, total, to be exact. And after that . . . well, I'm putting an end to all of this. It's gone on too long."

"So where are the submissions?" Winnie asked.

"You know that treasure chest I keep in my trophy

case? The piece I acquired on my trip to Scotland four years ago?"

The "piece"? Please. As in, "piece of junk"? Winnie nodded. "Yeah. Where did you move it?"

Olsen frowned. "Move it?"

"Yeah. Where?"

"I haven't moved it anywhere."

"Headmaster Olsen, you don't have to lie anymore, remember? We're in this together."

"I don't know what you're talking about," Olsen said.

Their gazes locked.

Oh my—

In a flash, the two of them were scrambling away from the desk, around the corner to the cellar door. The gray smog in Winnie's brain was thickening. Olsen shoved him aside and flew down the stairs, stumbling on the last couple of steps and nearly falling face first onto the basketball court. Winnie was right behind him, almost tripping over the old man's flaccid body. They staggered up to the trophy case.

"It's gone," Olsen gasped. He turned to Winnie, his hair flopping wildly. "Where did you put it? Where—"

"I didn't put it anywhere!" Winnie shrieked. He felt as if his chest were filled with hot smoke. "I thought you moved it!"

Olsen's eyes frantically roved over every inch of the trophy case, then across the entire basement, over every phony article, every fake award . . . and finally, when it was clear that the treasure chest wouldn't magically appear, his eyes welled with tears.

"They took it," Winnie whispered.

"Who?" Olsen asked, sniffling.

"All of them," Winnie said. "All—"

He was interrupted by a faint ringing sound upstairs.

The color drained from Olsen's face. "That's the doorbell," he said.

"Sal. Oh my God." Winnie's voice rose to a high-pitched wail. He couldn't help it. "That's Sal, isn't it?"

"Who else?" Olsen sobbed. "Who else?"

To: alums@wessex.edu
From: studentcouncil@wessex.edu
Subject: An Urgent Invitation

Dear Parents, Alumnae, and Friends of the
Wessex Academy,

We apologize for sending out a mass e-mail,
but given the gravity of the situation, we
felt it necessary. The Student Council
requests your company at an open forum to
discuss various issues affecting the school.
Please join us at 4 p.m. today, Wednesday,
October 24, 2001, at the residence of the
headmaster, 41 South Chapel Street.

Sunday Winthrop
Mackenzie Wilde
Allison Scott
Hobson Crowe
Noah Percy
Fred Wright*
* Newly appointed honorary Student Council
member

RSVP regrets only.
Casual attire.
Beverages will be served, and a brief film
will be shown.

13

Nobody seemed to be home.

Sunday poked the doorbell one more time.

"Can you please just tell us what this is about, Sunday?"

"I . . ." She glanced over her shoulder at her dad. His normally bland, cheery expression was gone. And he wasn't the only one who looked irritated. *All* the parents did. Mom, too. (Then again, Mom was missing her painting class, which was the high point of her week.) Sunday hadn't really expected so many parents to show up. But almost every one of them had answered the invitation. All except the Percys. And the Ellises, but they hadn't been invited. There must have been a good thirty people standing in front of Olsen's mansion: an impatient brigade of graying (Dad) or dyed (Mom) hair, Paul Smith blazers, Ralph Lauren sweaters, Laura Ashley dresses. . . . Even Carter Boyce's dad had showed, and that guy never left his estate in Darien. Rumor had it that he had three wives stashed there. One of them had supposedly had so much plastic surgery that she now looked exactly like Steven Tyler, the lead singer of Aerosmith.

Dad shook his head. "If this is such an urgent matter, why didn't Headmaster Olsen call us himself? I don't understand. I don't understand *any* of this, Sunday. The disappearing act Saturday night, concerned calls from teachers about your missing classes . . . frankly, this isn't like you at all. We've been very, very worried."

You're not the only ones, she thought.

"And if beverages are going to be served, then why wasn't this event catered as well?" Allison's mother asked.

The rest of the parents grumbled in agreement.

It suddenly occurred to Sunday that she really had no idea what she was doing. None of them did—not Fred, not Mackenzie, not Hobson, not Allison, or Noah. . . . Well, Noah still hadn't returned from his trip. For all she knew, he'd never even made it to the Cayman Islands. She glanced at the treasure chest in Hobson's hands. They still hadn't managed to get it open. They didn't know what was inside it. Maybe nothing. The plan had seemed so well-formed this morning, too: Gather all the parents together and expose Winslow Ellis and Headmaster Olsen for who they truly were, in person—after both of them had had a chance to review all the evidence against them. But after Winnie and Olsen had seen those files and read those letters, maybe they'd just taken off. Maybe *they* were in the Cayman Islands right now. Who was to stop them?

"Is this some kind of prank?" Allison's father demanded. "And why was Fred Wright's name included on the Student Council ledger?"

"You'll find out," Allison muttered. "Don't worry."

"I want to find out *now*," Hobson's dad growled. "I want to talk to Phil Olsen."

Sunday glanced at Fred. He shrugged. She rang the bell one last time. Still nothing. Her face was getting hot. She put her ear against the door.

A car screeched to a stop in front of the house. Sunday turned. It was a silver Rolls Royce—Mr. Percy's "big bucks ride," as he called it. A hushed murmur rose from the crowd as he slammed the car door and stormed up the front walk. He waved a letter in the air.

"What the hell is going on?" he demanded.

Nobody answered. Sunday stared at him. It was funny how much Noah looked like his father—the same slight build, the same curls—considering that Noah and his father had absolutely nothing else in common and were incapable of communicating. They couldn't even agree on a brand of shampoo. (According to Noah, anyway.) She shook her head. Inviting all these people here really *had* been a lousy idea.

"I said, what the hell is going on?" Mr. Percy asked again. "I just got a letter from my son saying that he was flying to the Cayman Islands. THE GODDAMN CAYMAN ISLANDS!" He shot an angry glare at Hobson. "Do you know anything about this? Can you tell me what in God's name has gotten into you kids? What's happening to this school?"

Hobson lifted his shoulders. "That's what I'm trying to find out, yo."

Sunday cleared her throat. "Listen, everybody, I know you're upset. I think the best thing for us to do would be to go around back and . . ." Her eyes narrowed.

Another car was screeching down South Chapel Street: A red Camaro. *Sal.* She shuddered. This was not good. If he was *here*, then Noah had probably never made it *there*—

Wait a second.

She squinted at the car windows as Sal pulled up behind Mr. Percy's Rolls. Sal wasn't alone. Noah was in the passenger seat. She let out a deep breath. He opened the door and pulled the seat up to let somebody out of the back. . . .

Sunday's lungs froze.

It was Mr. Burwell. Today's double-breasted suit was navy blue.

Her legs wobbled. She fell back against the door, unable to keep her balance. All at once she felt incredibly light-headed. No oxygen was flowing into her veins. She gaped at Sal as he pulled his own seat forward.

Miss Burke stepped out of the driver's side.

Hobson dropped the treasure chest. It bounced once on the lawn, ruining some of the sod.

"No way," Fred said. He backed up next to Sunday and squeezed her hand. "No way."

Sunday was extremely grateful that Fred had grabbed her, because if he hadn't, she would have keeled over and fainted. She forced herself to stand up straight.

Mr. Burwell and Miss Burke had been brought back to life.

It was a miracle. Well, either that or a horror show. Yes, definitely a horror show. Sunday had seen reruns of "The X-Files"; she'd listened to Mackenzie's rants about past-life regression therapy;

last winter, when she'd had the flu, she'd watched an entire season of "In Search Of"—this weird show from the '70s hosted by Mr. Spock from the original "Star Trek," which talked about the Bermuda Triangle and UFOs and, yes, even mummies and ghosts . . . but none of that came close to this in terms of sheer, unadulterated, terrible weirdness. She was staring at the resurrected. This was all the unexplained phenomena she could handle.

Tony Viverito was the last one out. He slammed the door.

Sunday finally managed to catch her breath. At least *his* appearance made *some* sense. At least *he* hadn't been *murdered*. Not that she knew of, anyway.

"Where have *you* two been?" Sunday's father asked, angrily looking from Mr. Burwell and Miss Burke. "I heard that you ran off together. On a Saturday night. When you should have been checking in students. I'd like you to know that I plan to write the board of trustees and ask that you be fired—"

"It's okay," Mr. Burwell interrupted. "We're resigning. I'm personally going to use the time to write a new screenplay. I have lots of material now."

"We're very sorry," Miss Burke said.

"It wasn't their fault," Sal added. "It was mine. I can explain everything."

Sunday turned to Fred. That was it. The proverbial

straw. She'd just seen two dead people hop out of a car—one of whom wanted to write a "new screen-play"—and Sal now sounded exactly like Noah's Uncle Adrian. But she was glad Sal had spoken up. Because *everybody* deserved an explanation. About *everything*. She took a deep breath, then marched across Olsen's front lawn, heading around the house to the backyard.

"Come on," she yelled.

Fred followed her.

Hobson grabbed the treasure chest and hurried after them.

Allison was next. Then Mackenzie. Then all the rest.

The back door was open, as always. And as Sunday marched through the kitchen and into the living room—leading the unruly, whispering, baf-fled throng of almost every single person she had ever grown up with, plus Fred—she realized some-thing. This was the very first time she'd broken into Olsen's house without feeling the slightest trace of guilt for doing something wrong or illegal. It *wasn't* wrong. Because if you thought about it, this wasn't really his house. It was the headmaster's mansion. It didn't belong to Olsen; it belonged to the Wessex Academy. And this group here—this *was* the Wessex Academy. Parents. Students. Teachers. Alums. The ones who ran committees. The ones who gave homework assignments. The ones who *did* homework assignments (most of the time). The ones who donated money for new facilities and ensured that this institution was among the finest preparatory schools in the nation—

"Hey," Fred said. "Do you smell that?"

Sunday paused in the foyer. She sniffed the air. It smelled faintly of burning leaves. She turned and glanced toward the cellar door. The odor grew stronger.

"The basement," they both breathed at the same time.

"Excuse me?" Allison's mother yelled from the back of the line. "If beverages are to be served, why haven't any preparations been made? Where is the help?"

Sunday dashed down the hall and threw open the door. Smoke wafted into her face. She coughed once, scowling, then hurried down the steps.

So. Olsen *was* home. And Winnie was with him. The two of them were standing in the middle of the basketball court, huddled over a small and very smoky bonfire made up entirely of white paper. They looked at Sunday.

She waved the smoke out of her eyes, blinking. "Isn't there something in the Orientation Handbook about not lighting fires on school grounds?" she asked.

"Page fourteen!" Noah yelled from the top of the stairs.

Winnie tried to stomp out the flames. It worked—but it also kicked up a swirling tempest of smoke and glowing embers and black ash . . . sort of what Sunday imagined a snowstorm in hell must be like. Hey! That was funny. Because now Olsen and Winnie pretty much had a snowball's chance in hell of talking their way out of whatever it was they were doing down here.

Something sharp nudged Sunday's back. It was Hobson's chest.

"Psst. Make room, yo," Hobson whispered.

Sunday stepped aside. The basement rapidly filled with coughing people, although most of the parents—wisely, no doubt—chose to remain upstairs. But Mackenzie's mom braved the smoke. So did Hobson's dad. And Noah's dad. And Sunday's dad. Sunday smiled. The plan was coming together. Not that she'd ever really had one.

Mrs. Wilde wandered over to the framed article that proclaimed Olsen the world's sexiest bachelor.

"So Phil," Mr. Crowe said. "Wouldn't a shredder have been safer than a fire?"

Olsen's jowls began to gyrate. He looked almost

exactly like a gobbling turkey. He glanced at Winnie, then back at the crowd, then at Winnie again.

"Good heavens, Phil," Mrs. Wilde said, peering at the article. "Julie Andrews? She was never your girlfriend."

"This is Winslow Ellis's fault!" Olsen shouted. He backed away from the fire and jerked a finger at Winnie. "He forced me to blackmail students because he found out I-I—I had a secret love of basketball—"

"He's lying!" Winnie shot back. "He's sick! He comes to students with these demented plans of ripping everybody off—"

"Winnie sells contraband on campus—"

"Phil kept the time capsule submissions." Winnie pointed at Hobson. A tear fell from his cheek. "He kept them all in there. He tricked kids into telling their secrets—"

"Whoa, chill," Hobson said. He looked down at the chest. "*That's* what's in this thing?"

Sunday laughed. Unbelievable. Maybe it was a good thing that Fred wasn't such an expert at picking locks. No, it definitely was a good thing. Because now, everybody's secrets were still safe. The way they should be.

The doorbell rang.

Sunday glanced back toward the stairs.

"Hey, you guys can shut up now," Sal Viverito called down from the first floor. "The cops are here."

It took about an hour or so for the cops—two very sweet young Connecticut state troopers, both of whom could have been Planet Biff's sons—to take statements from everyone. They spent most of their time talking to Sal.

Sunday couldn't believe how forthcoming he was about his role in the whole operation. He even turned over Noah's check as evidence. It was particularly beautiful, because Winnie's plastic surgery almost seemed to *melt* when he did it. Sunday was watching him the whole time. The reconstructed eyebrows again came together as one (a long yellow worm in the center of his forehead)—and his eyes were so puffy with tears that his faux cheekbones had vanished.

But still, even though Sunday was in an undeniably triumphant mood, she couldn't help but feel a little bittersweet, too. She'd known Winslow Ellis her entire life, after all. Maybe there was a soul in there, somewhere. Maybe a stay in prison would teach him—

Oh, stop it. What the hell was she thinking? The guy had about as much soul as a toolbox.

Sal told the cops to do whatever they wanted with

the check, but he mentioned that it would be nice if some of the money went to reimburse all the people Olsen and Winnie had ripped off. They told him they'd think about it, but chances were he'd end up being indicted for a variety of crimes, too—although they weren't exactly sure if impersonating a mobster was a violation of the criminal justice code.

And with that, the troopers handcuffed Olsen and Winnie and escorted them to the patrol car. Everybody followed them out onto the front lawn.

One of the cops opened the back door. "In you go, boys," he said.

Winnie shambled in without a word.

Sunday wrapped her arm around Fred's waist. He squeezed her back. *Remember this moment,* she reminded herself. *Remember that by helping send a jerk like Winnie to jail, you also forged a relationship with—*

All right. She was just going to have to stop thinking. Her own thoughts were too embarrassing. For *her.*

Olsen was next in line to get into the patrol car.

He ducked down, then hesitated, turning to face the crowd.

"Get in, G!" Hobson yelled. "This ain't no taxi service, yo!"

A couple of parents frowned at him.

Olsen cleared his throat. "I was only trying to

help the school," he announced. "I only wanted to raise money to build a first-rate, historically accurate reconstruction of an Elizabethan theater." He straightened, thrusting out his chest proudly. His bow tie was crooked, his hair a mess. "I leave you with an excerpt from *Henry the Eighth*."

Sunday stared at the ground. Okay. This was it. This was The Most Uncomfortable Moment of Sunday Winthrop's Life—all capitals. Why? Why did he have to embarrass himself like this? *Don't do this, Headmaster Olsen. Just get in the car—*

" 'Farewell!' " he cried. " 'A long farewell, to all my greatness! This is the state of man: Today he puts forth the tender leaves of hope; tomorrow blossoms, and bears his blushing honors thick upon him; the third day comes a frost, a killing frost, and when he thinks . . . he think . . .' " Tears started pouring down his cheeks, pooling in the folds of his jowls. " 'He thinks, good easy man, full surely his greatness is a-ripening, nips his root, and then he falls as I do. . . . And when he falls, he falls like Lucifer, never to hope again—' "

"Tell it to the judge, buddy," the cop interrupted. He shoved Olsen into the back seat and slammed the door, then rolled his eyes at his partner. The two of them hopped in and sped off down South Chapel Street, sirens wailing.

Nobody spoke for a long, long time.

Sunday sighed. Her arm fell away from Fred's waist. It was actually very peaceful on Olsen's front lawn. The sun was just beginning to set, and a cool autumn breeze was blowing.

"Well, I don't know about any of you," Sunday's father finally muttered, "but I could certainly go for a stiff vodka tonic right now."

"Here, here," Mackenzie's mother agreed.

"Where *are* the beverages?" Allison's mom asked.

Sunday shrugged. "We were just banking on the fact that Olsen usually has a stocked liquor cabinet," she said.

"And what about the film?" she asked. "Isn't there supposed to be a film?"

"It's this movie I have of Olsen doing Shakespeare in drag," Mackenzie said. "If you thought that his little performance just *now* was good, I bet you're all gonna freak about this one."

Hobson's father grinned. "That sounds like a good bet to me."

"Well, let's go then," Mr. Percy said. "I'll mix. Big bucks drinks, all around."

"You were always the best bartender," Sunday's mom said.

"They don't call me 'Big Bucks Chuck' for nothing."

"Ha, ha, ha!" went the parents. They began to file back into the house.

Fred took Sunday's hand.

"Sounds like a party's getting started," he said.

"It's about freaking time," she mumbled.

Sunday's dad paused in the doorway. He eyed Fred curiously. "I don't believe we've met," he said. "I'm Jonathan Winthrop, Sunday's father." He extended a hand. Sunday couldn't help but wonder if her dad was making the gesture just so Fred would stop holding *her* hand. Not that she really cared anymore. She was done caring.

"Fred Wright. Nice to meet you."

"You, too," Sunday's dad said. "So you're the star basketball player we've been hearing so much about."

Fred smiled. He took Sunday's hand again. "I used to be, anyway," he said wistfully.

Allison's mother poked her head back out the door. "Can I make a confession? When I received word of this gathering, I honestly thought it was to discuss the Harvest Ball."

"The Harvest Ball!" Sunday, Allison, and Mackenzie exclaimed at once.

Incredible. They all clamped their hands over their mouths. They'd all completely forgotten about it. But it was still scheduled for this Saturday night, the 27th of October. Invitations had yet to be printed. Then again, that was the Student Council's job, and, well . . . the Student Council had been pretty busy recently.

Noah looked at Hobson. "Who gives a crap about the Harvest Ball?" he muttered.

"It's a very important event, Noah," Allison stated.

"That's what they tell me." Noah gave Allison a quick up-and-down. "So what do you say? If they let me back in school, do you want to be my date?"

"What?" Allison cried. Her face turned pinkish. "*You?* I mean—not that—I just—"

"Well, why not? I figure Hobson's going with Mackenzie, Fred's going with Sunday. . . ." Noah glanced at Allison's mom. "You know, if that's okay with you, Mrs. Scott."

"Of course it is, dear." She smiled uncomfortably. "Why wouldn't they let you back in school? Are you in some sort of trouble?"

"Not anymore, I don't think," Noah said. He peered around the yard. "I don't see Miss Burke or Mr. Burwell around. . . ."

"They went to their faculty apartments to start packing," Fred said.

Mrs. Scott shook her head. "Heavens to Betsy. This is all a little too much for me."

"I know," Noah said. "Me, too. I'm just kidding,

Allison. The last thing I would ever want to do is to be your date. And I say that out of love."

"I-I—" Allison shook her head, too flustered to respond.

"Speaking of the Harvest Ball, what are you planning on wearing, sweetie?" Mrs. Scott asked.

Allison's teeth started grinding.

Sunday smiled. "How about the Lily Pulitzer?"

For a moment, Allison glared at her. Then her face softened. "I don't know. How about you?"

"I'm definitely going to wear it," Sunday said. "As long as you wear it, too."

Allison chuckled. "Well . . ."

"Then we can be twins again. Deal?"

"Deal," Allison said.

"Good." Sunday let go of Fred's hand and swept Allison into a quick, tight embrace. "I can't wait."

"Me neither," Allison breathed.

Sunday stepped back.

Good Lord. For about the billionth time in five days, she felt like crying. She'd better go get a V&T herself, and quick—so she could get drunk and start doing the hustle. Otherwise, she might start making a fool of herself.

"Cool," Noah said. "Chicks hugging chicks."

"Well, I don't know about you, but I'm gonna get me a beverage," Hobson said.

"Me, too," Mackenzie said.

"Me four," Noah said.

Fred pointed at the treasure chest, still tucked under Hobson's arm. "What are you going to do with that?"

"What do you think, yo? Bury it! Then twenty-five years from now, I'm gonna dig it up, bust it open, and read all the ill nonsense we wrote."

Sunday nodded. Finally. Somebody had a plan that, for once, made perfect sense.

Wessex Academy Class of 2002
Matriculation

Boyce, Carter : Harvard

Bryant, Hadley: Princeton

Crowe, M. Hobson III: Howard

Edward, Chase: Yale

Ellis, Winslow: Danbury Minimum Security Penitentiary

Mullins, Sarah: Parsons School of Design

Percy, Noah: Undecided/Year Off

Ramsey, Kate: Columbia

Scott, Allison: Dartmouth

Sutton, Boyce IV: Apex Technical Institute

Todd, Spencer: Vassar

Viverito, Anthony: Dartmouth

Wilde, Mackenzie: Amesbury Cairns College of Magick and the Forbidden Arts*

Winthrop, Sunday: Georgetown

Wright, Frederick: Georgetown

* Castle Fraser, Scotland